FOX

JOHN REINHARD DIZON

1

DEMON SEED

The old man had lived on this planet for over a hundred years. He resided in the village on this mountain upon which his ancestors dwelt since the beginning of time. His people gave birth to new generations, built homes, hunted and farmed, worshiped their gods, defended their land and buried their dead. He was a hunter/gatherer until he was too old to do so. He was now venerated as a shaman who shared the traditions of the past and interceded with the gods on the behalf of the village.

Over the past two decades there had been more frequent intrusions by the lowlanders. They came in packs with their firearms and spoke through interpreters. They warned of enemies who would steal, kill and destroy. They asked for volunteers to aid their cause. Sometimes the young, strong and adventurous would leave with them, never to return. Over time the village chief would order the youngsters to go into hiding until the intruders left. Yet there were always those who would follow them to the lowlands and never came back.

The older he got, the closer he got to the spirit creatures

and the gods. He saw visions and had strange dreams. The lowlanders waged war among themselves, and hundreds that died left their spirits behind. The spirits restlessly sought peace and roamed across the land. Some brought the evil that they had wrought throughout their lives. The old man would cast spells to drive them away.

As time passed, the vessels descended from the skies in greater frequency. Some would arrive to bring warriors and messengers from the heavens. The one that he saw this morning filled him with foreboding. This one was bringing with it great death and destruction. It was one with the swirling blade, the one that cast winds and made great noise. Normally it brought small groups of warriors. On this day it brought just one.

The old man prayed fervently that it was a gift from Xo.

The tall, auburn-haired man exited the helicopter and watched as it returned to the sky and disappeared. He tossed his duffel bag over his shoulder and crossed the small landing field on the way to the gravel road that was mentioned. It entered the treeline at a clearing where a young woman suddenly appeared.

"You must be Sergeant Mc Cain."

"So I'm told. And who might you be?"

"I'm Loki. I work at the camp."

She was a lovely Vietnamese woman standing five-four with a slender figure and a tight bosom. She wore a silk summer dress that clung to her body as a second skin. Her long black hair reached to her waist, and her almond eyes complemented her ruby lips.

"I'm sure you know I'm reporting for duty. Which way is best?"

"Let me see your left palm."

He raised his hand and she gently set hers beneath it.

"This is your map," she explained. "The short road leading west leads to the Eagle's Nest. The Lieutenant lives there. He is a spiritual man and guards the jungle area. He does not like to be disturbed. The next road to the right goes to Deadwood. It is where the Guardians reside. The middle road leads to Dogpatch, where the camp followers and villagers stay. South of that is the command post where the Captain controls all things. The last road leads to the Castle, where no one goes unchecked."

"Lots to unpack," he grinned. "Take me to your leader."

"Path Number Four," she pointed to the fourth dirt road leading down into a steep valley. "Good luck."

"So what'd you think of Loki?"

"Very attractive, very helpful."

Richard Mc Cain sat in a metal chair facing the desk of Captain Fred Federer. The CO (*commanding officer) ran the camp from a double wide trailer that was fashioned as a command post replete with wall maps, chalkboards, work stations and a large table sculpture in a far corner that replicated the landscape of the North-South border area of Vietnam. There was a small compartment in the opposite corner where Federer ate, rested and slept.

"She's quite a character. Personable, knowledgeable and resourceful. Just don't let her get too friendly, she'll play you like a harp."

Federer was a squat, chunky man with blue eyes that pierced through his bifocals. There was a streak of gray hair resembling a tuft of feathers that was combed back over his boulder-like skull. He smoked cigars from sunrise to sunset and only set one down in an ashtray when he had a point to make.

"I suggest you get changed, it's hell up here. You can use the restroom," Federer motioned at Richard's dress uniform. "You can leave your bag here while you admire the scenery. You can stay in the barracks or set up your own shop. Thing is, if you go shotgun shack, you'll be responsible for your spot along the perimeter."

"Roger that."

Richard changed into a dark green T-shirt, camouflage pants and combat boots, strapping his .44 Magnum to his belt and his bayonet to a calf sheath before heading down into the valley. Out of curiosity he decided to check out The Castle.

It was a single-wide trailer that was painted black, replete with tinted windows and black screens. A facade had been appropriated from an amusement park which made the front of the property appear as a castle with a drawbridge entrance and turrets on either side of the roof.

"Halt. Who goes there?" a voice came from a speaker horn at the entrance as he approached the drawbridge.

"It's the FNG (*Fucking New Guy)".

He heard a buzzer and entered the trailer as the door sprang shut behind him. It was a shadowy room lit by red light along the walls. A tall figure rose from a thickly-padded recliner along the far wall and came to greet Richard. They were as mirror images, standing six feet at two hundred ten pounds of muscle.

"Richard Mc Cain."

"Fritz Hammer."

"Quite an accent."

"I was about to say the same thing."

"St. Joseph, Missouri."

"Bismarck, North Dakota."

Richard took a seat on a sofa to the right of the recliner. The room temperature was comfortably set at seventy. Fritz pulled a bottle from a case by a night table and handed it to Richard.

"It's a home brew from the Old Country. I get a couple cases sent out every month. Out in the heat, a six pack will set you back on your heels."

"Great stuff," Richard took a swig and admired the chocolaty stout taste. He knew it came in around 40% alcohol.

"I take it you're looking for a place. Have you been to Deadwood?"

"Don't get me wrong, I'm a team player. I fight for the brand. Only I like being off by myself at times. This setup you got here is great. I'd like to hang my hat across the clearing if it's okay."

"No problem. I'll send the Crazy Eight to help. Tell them what you got in mind and they'll get it done. Anything you need, have them get your list to Loki. I'll cover the tab, just don't get carried away. We don't want to get off on the wrong foot. I'm sure a man like you knows how to stay on budget."

The Crazy Eight were two fire teams selected by Fritz as his personal combat unit. They were Bru Montagnards who had strong reputations among their people as hunters. They wore long black hair with copper-colored skin, stripped to the waist, clad in Army fatigues and combat boots. It amused Richard that they barely reached his shoulders in height. They were very friendly and were glad to take Richard's shopping list once it was completed. They bowed and grinned as they returned down the road back to the valley.

Richard set up a pup tent along the perimeter of the clearing. He set up a M-60 machine gun nest alongside his camp so as to honor the agreement. At the crack of dawn, he heard a sound and quickly rolled into the nest. He scanned the clearing and marveled at the sight of the Eight setting the foundation for his cabin almost noiselessly as to not disturb the sleeping commandos.

"So what've you got going there?" Fritz came out to his park bench with two cups of Irish coffee and two espressos.

"I want it to look like a carnival booth," Richard sat alongside him. "Fellows can come by and have drinks at the bar. I don't expect to be spending much time indoors, so I won't need much space."

"Those little guys work pretty fast," Fritz noted. "They should have you situated before dinner time."

Richard was used to having meals with the A Team wherever he had been stationed. Having his meals brought to him by caterers from Dogpatch was a novelty. He perceived that Fritz enjoyed his privacy, so did not offer to join him for dinner. He was indifferent as to dining alone. He had spent so much time alone while camping and hunting as a teenager that it did not matter.

The next morning, the repercussions were felt. There was a knock on the booth stand, and Richard came out to where Lieutenant Jim Tate stood.

Jim was a full-blooded Cherokee Indian. He had copper-colored skin and thick black hair that was two inches longer than Richard's. He was two inches taller at 6'2" and 240 pounds. There was a feral aura about him accentuated by his steely gaze, but his voice was surprisingly gentle.

"Looks like you got one of these," he nodded at Richard's doorpost as he waved a sheet of paper. Richard pulled it off and snickered at it.

"Are these people kidding?" Fritz came over from The Castle with his own document. "This is old school green beanie crap."

"I'm thinking they're feeling like we're being snobbish," Jim

6

replied, shaking hands with Fritz. Richard sensed a strong bond of respect between them.

"A summons," Richard chuckled. "Now I've seen everything."

"Well, we'd best go in together. We can act as each others' advocates," Jim smiled.

"I'll give them a fricking advocate," Fritz growled.

"Now, now," Jim chided. "All for one and one for all."

They made their way down into the valley along Path Two. There was a small dirt clearing bracketed by wooden shacks resembling a Wild West hamlet. Fritz led them onto the boardwalk where Betty's Battalion sat.

Betty was the widow of an Army lieutenant whose saloon in Saigon was destroyed by the Viet Cong during the Tet Offensive. III Corps officers met with her and explained that they would be unable to fully compensate her for her losses. They did advise her of opportunities in I Corps near the village of Dong Ha. Despite the admonitions of her relatives, she accepted the offer and opened a new saloon in Deadwood.

She was an attractive though crusty woman who rarely smiled. She had four barmaids and two bartenders who helped her handle the rowdy customer trade. She nodded toward the rear of the table area where eight Green Berets in their fatigues awaited at a row of tables joined together. The three invitees took seats at separate tables, facing the teammates.

"We're taking a ride down to Saigon this Friday," Jerry Brown spoke up. He was a massive albino with a Cajun drawl, easily a physical match for Jim. "We want you with us but we'll be showing our colors. You fellows will need to get patched."

"I've already got a patch on my beanie," Fritz sneered.

"C'mon, get with it. You been spending too much time in your ivory tower," Jerry growled.

"Ivory?" Fritz looked from Jim to Richard. "It was black the last time I looked."

"We haven't rolled down there since Tet," Jerry replied. "We got business with the jarheads and we don't want to look weak. Everyone knows the situation with Fred. Only we asked you nice last time, Jim, but you had that Injun thing you were playing."

"You're not dissing my thing, are you, Jerry?" Jim was menacing.

"C'mon, guys, where's the team spirit?" Steve Korn spoke up. He was the communication specialist, a cherubic man of Jewish descent. "Look, I had no plans to join a biker gang. I just wanted to fit in. The initiation wasn't pretty, but I'm glad I got through it."

"Okay, let's get this over with," Fritz feigned a yawn. "We can run a gauntlet. I'm just letting you know up front. If you fellows get carried away, at least a couple of you will end up in the infirmary."

"Not this time," Jerry grinned wickedly. "The guys you replaced trained with the LURPs (*USMC Long Range Reconnaissance). They drove it in deep and hard. Now, Jim, we know you and the Yards have been doing some heavy stuff out there past the Minefield, and we respect that. Same with you, Fritz. Now, Mc Cain, we know you built a rep during Tet. Fifty registered kills, I hear."

"More like a hundred, as I recall," Mc Cain was casual.

"A hundred!" Jerry howled. "*Je l'aime!*"

"Here's the deal," George Bullski, a swarthy Chicagoan, narrowed his eyes. "It's what the Injuns call counting coup. I don't think Jim should have a problem bringing us back a scalp. Maybe he can show Fritz how to do it. If Mc Cain's not up to it, we can let him ride along as a prospect until he passes muster."

"So you're gonna turn this into an Indian thing," Jim blazed.

"No, no, no," Fritz held up a finger. "I got this."

"No, *I* got it," Richard gave George an icy smirk. "We'll have your souvenirs first thing in the morning."

"Listen, Mickey---" Fritz sidled over to him.

"*You* listen, Squarehead. I got this."

The meeting ended as a tense atmosphere prevailed. The three men left the saloon after politely declining a round of drinks. Jim bade the two farewell as he headed back to The Nest. Fritz and Richard returned back up the slope to Path Five.

"Want me to send the Crazy Eight?" Fritz asked before retiring.

"I know where to find them. See you tomorrow."

Richard had a vision that evening of his great-grandfather, Henry Geronimo, leading him along the dirt road past the Minefield towards the DMZ. Grandpa was in blackface, clad in black fatigues, carrying an exotic bow and arrow sheath. He remained far ahead of Richard, using hand signals to coordinate their movement. They moved further and further into enemy territory until, in the utter blackness, Richard fell down a rabbit hole.

He plummeted for what seemed as centuries until at last he landed in a jello-like substance along a midnight landscape. As he struggled to his feet, he realized it was clotted blood. He wiped his eyes and could see bloody skeletons rising from the gore to surround Grandpa. The diminutive warrior fought valiantly, severing limbs, slicing off heads and separating torsos. He chopped down over a dozen before he turned to Richard and spoke telepathically:

This is what you must do.

At once the ground exploded as a blackish mountain rose at

Grandpa's feet before he disappeared. Richard staggered erect and saw bloodied skulls spewing from the mountain as from a volcano. The mountain became a pile of skulls, hundreds of thousands tumbling from within. At length a flagpole rose to end the flow at the peak, and from it an American flag unfurled.

Do us proud, my son. Do us proud.

Richard passed into unconsciousness.

At the crack of dawn, the residents at the barracks in Deadwood heard a commotion at the door. Jerry Brown cursed the slopes for sleeping on duty. He rolled out of his bunk and opened the door, puzzled by the large sack at the doorstep.

At his feet were eight heads in a duffel bag.

It was around noon when word arrived at the Castle that Richard, Fritz and Jim would be receiving their patches at Betty's Battalion that evening. Richard stopped by the Castle and had a seat at the brass-wrought coffee table by the sofas where they sat.

"Thought I'd give you a taste, see what you think," Fritz nodded towards the works sitting atop the table. It was a syringe along with a spoon, a lighter, a rubber tube and a packet of heroin.

"Nope, not for me," Richard said then squinted at Fritz. "Somehow I didn't take you for the type."

"Just checking," Fritz picked up a trash basket and swept the items off the table with his hand. "I was wondering if you'd be interested in a business opportunity."

"You're just full of surprises today."

"It's not like we're earning a fair wage for what we do," Fritz leaned back on the sofa. "And there's no workman's comp. Lots of guys going home in baskets wish there was something they could've set aside. Do you have anyone back in the World?"

"Well, I've got an older brother with a wife I'd do something for. How about you?"

"My parents are still alive," Fritz nodded.

"So what's the angle?"

"You know the VC lifeline is the Ho Chi Minh Trail," Fritz steepled his fingers. "MACV (*Military Assistance Command Vietnam) devotes half of the campaign to closing it down. They tear up one smuggling route, two others take its place, like a Hydra. What the VC can't inject into their network they send up to North Vietnam. MACV either destroys what is captured or returns it to the South Vietnamese. The rest ends up on the black market."

"Yeah, I've been around, Seen and heard all of it."

"I got a guy getting patched up at the hospital in Saigon," Fritz revealed. "He's got connections with the network shipping dope back Stateside. Only his movers are having problems with a VC-connected crew setting up shop downtown. The crew also has connections with the Saigon Police. The fellow's action is getting shut down and he needs someone to sort things out."

"Are you serious?" Richard furrowed his brow. "How'd you get caught up in all that?"

"I'm not," Fritz assured him. "I'm more of a day trader. Now and again I take the Crazy Eight out on recon and we come across a hijack gang. I have a source at the Marine base who trades on the take. I get enough to have a couple of cases of dark beer shipped from Bavaria. I send the rest to my Swiss bank account. The Yards chip in and have a truckload of canned goods sent up the mountain."

"Okay, I'll take a look," Richard agreed.

· · ·

The ceremony went as scheduled, and Richard, Fritz and Jim were given their patches. The biker club was called the Guardians. The patch featured the name on a sash above an angel wearing a cross holding a sword and a rifle. They were sewn onto extra large cutoff denim jackets, all of which fit the three commandos just right.

They were gifted with Harley-Davidsons, which greatly impressed them. Only they were told they would have to relinquish them should they be transferred or killed. It took some of the luster off, but it was an ego boost nonetheless. They fit in perfectly as the bikers mustered at Betty's that Friday morning. They went inside for boilermakers before hopping on the bikes and sailing down the road to Saigon.

It was an anticipated event as there were helicopter and recon jet sorties crossing overhead along Route 9 at regular intervals. Richard was aware of the Green Beret 'mafia', how business was conducted and things were arranged. Only in Saigon it was similar to military politics back home. Here seemed to be much different. The branches were connected to the civilian and underground networks, and they dealt behind the scenes like cops and robbers back home. Only this was going on amidst a terrible war, and Richard was certain this would be an experience like no other in the coming months.

It was a twelve-hour ride to Saigon, and night had fallen before they arrived. Gunshots and explosions could be heard in the jungle in the distance. Only the aerial cover continued, and they coasted into town without incident. The streets were bustling with activity as cars and trucks carried soldiers and civilians to and fro. Peddlers hawked their wares in the streets and hustlers solicited pedestrians at regular intervals.

"Okay, guys, we meet back here tomorrow morning at noon," Jerry rolled his bike over to where Richard, Fritz and Jim came to a halt. The twelve bikes sat in front of a large fountain in the middle of the city. "Everybody's got appointments somewhere or other. Some get paid, some get laid, some get high, but nobody dies. Stay outta trouble."

"I've gt some connections with FULRO I need to check out," Jim told them. "I'll see you two back here. If you have a problem, call this number."

"FULRO?" Richard perused the card printed in French.

"Front Unifie de Lutte des Races Opprimees," Fritz explained. "The United Front for the Liberation of Oppressed Races. The Yards are a minority here, they're like the blacks back home. FULRO started in Cambodia and made its way here in '65. Jim sees them as kindred to the Indians in America. That's why he keeps to himself. The Vietnamese call the Yards *moi*, savages. Jim gets pissed, it creates tension."

"Yeah, like that crap going on in Northern Ireland," Richard grunted. "Makes no sense."

"Okay, let's go pay my boy a visit."

The Saigon Hospital operated at a frantic pace, 24/7. Military casualties were brought in alongside trauma victims, overdose patients and those with various illnesses. Preferential treatment was rampant and only those with connections or life-threatening injuries were kept at the facility. Sgt. Walter Green had been there for a week.

Richard and Fritz arrived at the fifth floor and came to room 513 where two black gunmen sat guard outside. They identified themselves and were permitted entry. Green was in bed, his head, arms and torso heavily bandaged. An IV bag was attached to his left arm.

"Well, you've looked better," Fritz grinned. "Looks like you did something for your country for a change."

"Fuck you, squarehead potato-eating motherfucker," Green snarled.

"Seems like someone should have finished the job," Fritz

drew his Mauser from his side holster and pointed it at Green's forehead. They heard triggers being cocked behind them and Richard turned to the gunmen to defuse the situation.

"Come on, fellows, we're here to do business, or so I thought. Should we go back outside and start over?

"No, we're already acquainted," Fritz holstered his pistol. "So what is it that you couldn't handle?"

"Wouldn't have been no problem if my unit hadn't run into a VC ambush," Green scowled. "That mofo Giao Long opened up an underground casino downtown and set up shop after Tet last year. He got connections with the police and don't get hassled. He got backup from the VC, and when they step in to squash a beef they step hard. He took over the gambling, then the whores. Now he trying to get the drugs and the black market trade. The jarheads I work with was gonna step in, but Saigon Special Branch been watching them. They telling me if I can't get the pipeline clear, they gonna go somewhere else. There's too much competition. I'm going out of business if we can't get this problem solved."

"All right," Fritz nodded. "Give me an address, I'll go talk to your jarhead friends."

"And don't go in there with no attitude or pull no off-the-wall shit like you do here," Green warned. "These mofos don't be messing around."

Buffalo Bill was a sergeant major who had served in Korea and was considered the go-to guy in the Marine network at Saigon. He had strong connections with the LURPs and kept a squad on hand at his warehouse headquarters. He was a massive veteran who had a reputation for skinning his victims alive to resolve gang wars and turf disputes.

"So Beat Shit Green sent you two out to handle his

problem," Bill narrowed his eyes at them. They stood before his command table on the grade floor of the shadowy warehouse, They were flanked by two riflemen carrying M-16s.

"He said you direct traffic out here," Fritz replied airily. "I hope you can get us going ASAP. I got a long ride back to the DMZ tomorrow."

"You work the DMZ?" Bill seemed somewhat impressed. He wrote out instructions on a sheet of paper and passed it across the desk. "You guys change back there in the store room. You'll go out with two of the Yards. One'll go with you, the driver stays outside. He'll wait for as long as it takes. If you don't come out, he comes back alone. I don't want them grabbing our vehicle and running checks."

The Golden Dragon was located in the basement of the Vietnamese Goods and Storage Warehouse. It was known that motorcycle cops patrolled the area and routinely pulled vehicles over for random checks. There were passwords for those allowed access to the back alley where the entrance was located behind the building. The driver gave the password to a bike cop after being pulled over and was granted passage.

The black Citroen pulled over down the block from the entrance and allowed Richard and Fritz to exit. Their escort, Ca Ki, led them to the doorway where they were frisked by two hulking Samoan guards. They followed Ki down a dark corridor leading to the raucous gambling den.

"You look like shit," Richard chuckled. They both wore Hawaiian shirts, blue jeans and tennis shoes, appearing as civilian tourists.

"Yeah? Well, at least they washed *my* shirt."

The casino served as a notorious betting site for Russian roulette matches. Contestants sat across a poker table from one another, taking turns pointing a revolver at their temples and pulling the trigger. There was one bullet in a six-cylinder chamber which was spun and loaded before the match. The audience bet heavily on the match, the winner being declared when the opponent fired the gun and blew his brains out.

Ki stepped up to the manager and told him that the white men wished to participate. He explained that they were business rivals who wanted to settle old scores. He also informed the man that Richard had a terminal illness and that Fritz's wife had left him for another man. They had planned this and did not intend to leave together.

The manager scurried to the rear area where a debonair man was surrounded by men wearing suits. The gold-embroidered dinner jacket identified him as Giao Long, the Golden Dragon himself. The manager told him of the situation, and Long gladly agreed. The patrons were always eager to see white men blowing their brains out instead of their fellow Vietnamese. Having them compete against one another increased the excitement. Bettors waged top dollar, and the winners would spend more than usual when the tables reopened after the matches.

Richard and Fritz sat down across from one another, placing a stack of bills in front of them. The crowd could see the one hundred dollar American bill at the top of each stack. The referee stepped up, made an announcement, then loaded and rolled the barrel of a pistol before slamming it down on the table between the stacks. He spun it like a wheel three times before the barrel finally came to a stop in pointing at Richard.

He exhaled heavily before picking the pistol up and staring at it. Suddenly he leaped to his feet and began fanning the hammer, a shot resounding throughout the room. Giao Long's skull exploded as a can of tomatoes, his brains spewing from the back of his head across the floor behind him. Fritz ripped the bands from the stacks of bills and overturned the table, causing the cash to cascade across the platform. The patrons began vaulting over the barricades to grab the money, which was dollar bills beneath the hundred on top.

Bedlam ensued as a mob scene unfolded. The two men grabbed beer bottles and broke off the necks as they followed Ca Ki to the exit. The Samoans saw what happened and blocked their escape. Richard threw a groin kick at the first man before driving the bottle neck into his jugular vein. He glanced at Fritz, who had plunged the glass into his adversary's eyeball. They raced out behind Ki and jumped into the Citroen, which sped off into the darkness.

"Well, that's a hard day's night," Richard grinned as they caught their breath.

They returned to Buffalo Bill's headquarters and gave back the Hawaiian shirts. They put their Guardians vests back on, hopped on their bikes and found a motel where they spent the night. By noon they met with the team at the city fountain as agreed. They had slept in and were bright eyed and bushy tailed for the long ride back to Dong Ha.

Beat Shit Green's connection was restored shortly thereafter.

2

HAMLET

The Vietnamese Resettlement Program was designed to relocate people whose villages had been destroyed by marauding Viet Cong forces. It was managed by State headquarters in Saigon and proved as corrupt as every other governmental agency. The Americans could see a pattern of citizens having connections being assigned to communities close to Saigon and other urban areas in III and IV Corps. Women, children and the elderly were shipped to villages at I and II Corps in jungle areas distant from heavily populated areas. Dong Ha was seeing more and more of these refugees.

Dogpatch was what was considered a fortified hamlet. Its citizens constituted a militia force supervised by the Luc Luong Dac Biet (*Vietnamese Special Forces) whose village was as a fort dedicated to protecting the area from Communist troops. The RFPF (*Regional Forces/Popular Forces) lived in the hamlet along with their immediate family. Similar to the State of Israel, the women and children often fought alongside the militia when the hamlet was under attack.

Captain Federer faced a chronic challenge of coordinating

the activities of the Special Forces A-Team with the LLDB, who they scorned as their designated counterparts. The LLDB vainly attempted to replicate the A-Team, which included disrespecting the RFPF just as they were derided. The ARVN (*Army of the Republic of Vietnam) were equally despised by the A-Team and the LLDB, but the attitude could only travel so far along the chain of command. The RFPF had no such insulation.

"We've got to get this new RFPF team up to speed, there's no other choice," Federer exhorted the team as they held their Monday morning meeting at his office. "Lives are at stake here, it needs no explanation. You need to play nice with the LLDB and make this happen. Bring in some of the top rank ARVNs if you have to."

"And could you tell us who those might be?" Jerry Brown asked, to a raucous chorus of laughter.

"Okay, look," Fred puffed his cigar like a locomotive when upset. "There's been a lot of VC activity in the jungle near the Cambodian border as of late. MACV thinks they're up to something. We don't want to take the chance of them carving a path across the jungle and hitting the hamlet before it's ready. If it happens and there's a massacre, the Major comes after me and he reports to the Colonel. That goes to General Westmoreland, and I end up taking a ride to Saigon. That's not on my agenda, and you better make sure it stays that way."

"Fuggin' Ruff and Puffs (*RFPF)," Jerry growled as he joined Richard, Fritz and Jim outside after the meeting. "I got enough with the Low Life Dick Brains (*LLDB) this week. Look, you gotta help me out here. It's like being the ringmaster having to train a new batch of midgets at the circus."

"All right," Fritz frowned. "Mickey, why don't you give him a hand?"

"Sure thing, Square," Richard shot back. "And what may I ask will you be up to?"

"Sounds like Grandpa and I'll be beating the bush all week," Fritz replied.

"You got it, Square," Jim delighted in the new nickname Richard gave Fritz.

"You're going out in daylight?" Jerry was surprised. "I thought the jarheads were handling that."

"If they were, we wouldn't be going out, would we?" Jim replied gruffly.

Fritz and Jim worked with the Montagnard volunteers who regularly came down from the mountains. Their quarters were located on either side of the Valley, providing security on the east and west perimeters. The VC knew of their locations by the Minefield facing the DMZ and remained cautious. Their attacks on the outposts had been met with ferocity and horrific reprisals. They adopted a live and let live attitude toward the camp, venting their frustrations against the Marines at the Dong Ha Combat Base.

Richard resigned himself to working with the LLDB and the RFPF though he would have rather accompanied Fritz. He trudged down Path Two on Tuesday morning, dressed in his T-shirt and fatigues. He saw the roped-off areas where the LLDB had assembled the RFPF, and spotted members of the A Team working alongside the LLDB. They were practicing martial arts, which proved of vital importance when faced with hand-to-hand combat against the VC. Charlie (*Victor Charlie) was poorly trained and often proved incompetent in such scenarios.

He sauntered over to where Jerry Brown was working with a dozen RFPF recruits. Jerry was the first to arrive and among the first to leave due to the effect the Vietnamese sun would have on his alabaster skin. He appeared as a giant vampire, gleefully slinging three of the peasants around at one time. They picked themselves up from the dirt and circled him, seeking an opening. Only he was as a cat toying with mice, snatching one at random and slamming him to the ground. The workout paused long enough for the man to regain his feet and resume, groggy as he might be.

"Mc Cain," Jerry spotted him and waved him down. "C'mon over and take a shot at it. You can show the dinks how it's done."

"Sure thing," Richard stepped over the rope into the squared area. He took his shirt off as had Jerry to avoid giving an opponent a handhold. He knew this was a test, and approached it with vigor. The recruits thankfully left the cordon as the commandos squared off.

They simultaneously broke into horse stances, circling about as giant crabs. Richard moved in and threw a flurry of left jabs. Jerry stepped out of range before closing in and throwing three crisp roundhouse kicks. Richard timed the kicks and grabbed Jerry's leg on the third try. He was pleasantly surprised by the man's agility as he sprang off the ground and fired a left roundhouse, using Richard's leglock as an anchor. Richard rolled with the blow, then rolled again and grabbed Jerry in a headlock. Again Jerry excelled in slipping the lock and rolling around to straddle Richard. Mc Cain reached across with his right hand, grabbing the powerful left clutching the back of his neck. He twisted with all his weight, trapping Jerry's hand as he continued to roll. Jerry's wrist was compromised and he had no way to prevent Richard from scissoring his left arm and forcing him to tap out.

"Damn, that was a good move," Jerry shook his left arm out. "Gimme a couple of minutes, we can try it again."

"Better yet," Richard retrieved his shirt. "I take six, you take six. We'll coach them and see who's got the best teaching style."

"Huh," Jerry glanced around at the intimidated recruits. "Yeah, that could work. How about we put twenty bucks on it?"

"Okay. Patch honor, though. If we start bickering over the score, all bets are off."

"Done."

They spent a half hour instructing their teams before the bouts began. Richard and Jerry were as boxing managers yelling instructions as the fights commenced. The commotion attracted the other A-Team members as well as the LLDB. They thought it was a great idea, and soon the entire exercise field was filled with new enthusiasm as the team competition began to spread.

Jerry took his leave by noon as the sun began to beat down. Richard allowed the group to retire and went over to the water station for refreshment.

"Sir, I was asked to introduce myself," a bespectacled Vietnamese soldier approached. "I am Pin Pon, your LLDB counterpart. Your mirror, as they say."

"The hell you say," Richard snorted. "I've never been that ugly."

"They asked that I humbly invite you to accompany me to the hamlet. Dogpatch, as they call it. I understand you haven't been there yet."

Pon reminded him of the Chinese people he met back in Missouri. They were stoic, impassive yet humble in demeanor. Only the Vietnamese seemed more subjective in contrast to the rationality of the Chinese. The Viets seemed to absorb everything, taking all into a spiritual account. In that they seemed far more enigmatic. Yet their energy release could be astounding and frightening, as evidenced by the Viet Cong.

He considered Jim's relationship to the Montagnards. The

Native American shared the impassivity of the Chinese. Yet many had an aura of bridled tension that could explode at any moment. Henry Geronimo was like that. It was why they were forbidden strong drink in some areas of America. When they lost control, like the Viet Cong, it could result in chaos and tragedy. Only the Yards were even more passive and reserved than the Viets. Perhaps that was where the enmity lied. People often project their hate upon others when they reflect the things they abhor about themselves.

"They suggest you visit the schoolhouse," Pon offered as they arrived at the hamlet, located along the outskirts of Dogpatch. Richard considered the fact that it was not dissimilar to other villages. It consisted of long rows of thatched huts separated at intervals by aluminum storage depots. He was often bemused by the disdain of Americans and Europeans for the primitive ambiance. Yet if these same huts were located along the coasts of Blue Hawaii, they would sacrifice a month's pay to rent them for vacation use.

They entered the schoolhouse where a Maryknoll nun was giving the children an English lesson. There were six rows of five desks, and the children were greatly excited to see the visitors. They stood quietly as the nun greeted the soldiers, followed by their own chorus of 'good morning'. She told the children to be seated, then Pon introduced them before asking Richard to speak.

"We're delighted to see you children here in attendance," Richard smiled. "Work hard, do your best, and follow your dreams. Your parents are sacrificing so that you can carry on their traditions and live in peace and liberty. The American people support their cause, and together we will see Vietnam realize a bright new future."

Richard and Pon returned to Dogpatch where they left on cordial terms. He trudged back to The Castle where Fritz had just returned. He was invited inside where they had a couple of beers before retiring for the afternoon.

He had long known that SOG (*Special Operations Group) was handled differently than most under MACV, which was a mistake. Even long distance runners in the World spent most of their time resting and recuperating before marathons. Special Forces troops devoted much of their day to eating, sleeping and hydrating. Sending Army and Marines out for long hikes in this brutal weather was outlandish. Together with the horrific violence, culture shock and physical trauma, it was no wonder that drug and alcohol abuse was so rampant. Men returned to the World as broken shells of their former selves. The military owed them far better.

Waking at daybreak was par for the course. Fritz had coffee waiting by the drawbridge, and Richard joined him as was the new routine.

"There was a bit of commotion over by Cam Lo yesterday," Fritz revealed. "You know about the VC's 27th Battalion going up against the Marines' 2nd Battalion and getting their arses whipped back in February. I think they're planning to start some more shit. I was wondering if you'd like to run down with us to the new hamlet and make sure things are okay."

"Never thought you'd ask."

"Okay, here's the thing. We move fast and we move hard. Brute speed. But we're big cats, they never know we're coming. The Yards run the lead, they always go first. They've been working the bush since they were old enough to walk. Plus they're smaller and faster than you. You got to follow my lead at all times because we've got a system worked out. We stay together. If I go down or we get separated, you retreat back here. If you don't, rest assured you go home in a bag."

"Wow," Richard marveled. "Damn."

"That's the way it's gotta be, or you can forget we had this conversation. I work alone. Uncle Fred knows it. You can go out with Jim, or the Team if you prefer."

"Aye, aye, Captain Crook," Richard gave him a middle-finger salute.

"Good. Go get your shit, we leave in a half hour."

The Crazy Eight met them at the clearing from where they entered the jungle trail heading south. Both Richard and Fritz carried AK-47s, with their pistols on their hips and machetes on their calves. Richard also had a sawed-off Remington 870 strapped to his left thigh. They also had rucksacks on their backs which held ammo and grenades. The Yards resembled American Indians, dressed only in loincloths carrying bows and arrow sheaths. They had white paint smeared over their bodies, the commandos wearing camouflage paint on their faces.

Richard was reassured by the traditional formation as they sallied forth. Four of the Eight walked the point at a ten-yard distance from right to left, front to rear. Two Yards preceded them and two walked behind, the pairs at a five yard distance. Considering the prowess of the team members, it would have been almost impossible to ambush them in this environment.

As they moved through the heavy foliage, their pace slowed as they relied on the point guards in progressing. The Yards had a clicking whistle sound with which to communicate that could have been easily mistaken for an exotic bird. The column proceeded when they could see a hand signal from the point guards. They would carefully move forth until they lost sight of the point men. They then waited for the clicking sound and crept ahead until the hand signal appeared once again.

When they arrived along the outskirts of the hamlet, they were greeted with an eerie silence. Fritz signaled and they spread into a skirmish line in the foliage. Y Gal, the bravest of the Eight, crouched and sprinted with feline stealth across the clearing to the nearest hut. Richard and Fritz trained their rifles on the hut as Y Gal crept around the side.

"Suppose he's trapped?" Richard whispered.

"It never happens," Fritz hissed. "If it does, two more follow him in. If they don't come back, we move in with grenade pins pulled."

Tense minutes elapsed before Y Gal reappeared. He gave a signal and the point men began creeping toward the hut. They spread slowly onto the village court, giving sign to the rest as they walked ahead. Richard and Fritz followed the hunters into the hamlet and were astounded by what they saw.

The Viet Cong had attacked the village and massacred its residents. The bodies of the children had been dismembered, the body parts cast onto the main road. As all the young men were training at Dong Ha, the elderly had their skulls caved in. The women had either been raped or their private parts mutilated before their throats were slit. This included the Maryknoll nuns who were servicing the inhabitants. All the storage huts were set ablaze.

"I'm gonna make them wish they'd never left the womb," Fritz was apoplectic.

"All right," Richard gripped his forehead. "Let's think this through. The blood's not dry, even with the heat. This had to have happened about an hour ago. They can't have gone far. We know they didn't go north. They're not headed for the seashore, for sure. If we sent an alert, the south would be swarming with choppers. They're headed for the Cambodian border. We can catch them."

"Y Mac," Fritz called the leader of the point guards over. The hunters were distracted by the carnage, wandering around numbly. Some were on their knees pleading with their gods. "We're moving out west after the bastards. I want you fellows to stay sharp. Block this out, we'll have our turn. Do nothing until I say so. Even if you come across a gang rape, you check back with me first."

Once again they were as an invisible hand groping the jungle as they set out in pursuit of the enemy. They were moving at a swifter pace, but Richard was not overly concerned. They knew that the VC would be hurried in their retreat. It was also less likely they would set up an ambush for a pursuing force. The enemy would be expecting a large and aggressive counteroffensive if one was indeed mounted in such a short time. It would make them less concerned or expectant of a smaller team as this.

Richard admired the efficacy of the hunters as they swept through the foliage like phantoms. After a hand signal and a series of clicks, Y Ste fell back to where Richard and Fritz awaited. He reported that he found signs of fresh blood at the forward right point. The enemy could not be very far ahead of them.

"I take it these fellows know their roles," Richard whispered. "We may well be running into a platoon. There had to be at least forty victims back there."

"Don't worry, they're not new at this by a long shot," Fritz grinned wickedly. "They were born for moments like these."

They had traveled over an hour before both forward guards reappeared without hand signals. Richard immediately dropped to his knee and readied his rifle. He had seen the VC routinely slaughter victims and set up traps for pursuing teams. If the hunters had been compromised, this would be a life-or-death shootout.

"They have a visual," Fritz dropped down alongside him. "Stay with me, we're going to the set-up."

Richard watched as the point guards came together, then followed each other into the bushes heading to the right. The other four hunters waited for a minute before slipping forward and disappearing into the brush.

"Give them a minute, then we go," Fritz advised him. "Stay close, this can hit the fan at any second."

Fritz counted to sixty in German before leading the way into the foliage. They crept stealthily until they heard an anxious exchange of conversation in Vietnamese up ahead. They realized they had caught up to the Viet Cong.

They moved forward breathlessly until they could see the group in the clearing ahead. There were about two dozen, standing apart in groups of six. Two of the men seemed to debating their next move. Both commandos understood Vietnamese and knew they were arguing whether to split their forces or continue as a group toward the border. Some were washing blood from their clothes and weapons with canteen water so as not to attract mosquitoes or beasts of prey.

"Don't make a move until I say," Fritz whispered.

"Hey, this isn't my first rodeo."

"No matter. If any of the Yards get killed, the tribe'll get pissed at me and not show up for a couple of days. Not how I want to end the day."

At once they were astonied as Y Zwo stepped out of cover, holding his bow at his side as he appeared before the VC. The enemy was equally dumbfounded before one of the riflemen stepped behind the hunter and grabbed him by the hair.

"What are you doing here, you dumb son of a bitch?" the leader demanded.

"I was stalking a deer," he replied meekly. "Did you see where he went?"

The VC recovered sufficiently to break out in relieved laughter.

"I'll tell you what, you stupid bastard," his lieutenant

snarled. "How about us catching a tiger? We'll cut your head off and see if that lures one in."

"How about this," they heard the feral tone of a native Missourian speaking in barbaric Vietnamese. "We'll cut all your balls off and see if we can start a menagerie."

The leaders started to cry out but were left speechless by Montagnard arrows protruding from their chests. Richard and Fritz charged from the bush, their machetes whirling as propeller blades as they charged the unsuspecting VC. The hunters fired their arrows as fast as they could set their bows, and the guerrillas began falling as timber logs. Some tried to draw their pistols but had their hands chopped off by the attackers. Others had their arms hacked off. Yet some stumbled backward toward the Montagnards, necks spouting fountains of blood from where their heads had been.

It was over almost as soon as it began. The hunters surveyed the carnage and were satisfied that the VC had reaped what they had sown. Body parts were strewn everywhere, and the ground was as soggy as if it had rained blood.

"Looks like we're done here," Richard assessed. "Might as well head back to the village and call in the Marines."

"Not by a damn sight," Fritz snarled. "Y Gal, have the boys cut me some bamboo shoots. We'll let the VC come on out and think about pulling a stunt like this again."

The team returned to the hamlet and were nettled by the sight of dogs, cats and swine gnawing at the corpses. They swatted at them as they searched for radio equipment, calling the Dong Ha Combat Base for reinforcements. They left after making the call, and soon heard the sound of choppers coming from north and south. Richard made the call and explicitly described their return path so as not to get hit by friendly fire.

The Green Berets and the rest of the camp were in a forlorn mood after news of the massacre was announced. They mourned the loss of life, exacerbated by the desecration of the nuns though the women, children and elderly were just as grievous a loss. Although the hamlet was within the jurisdiction of the Marine base, MACV would lay the blame on the SOG.

The team was entirely unaware of the retribution that Richard and the boys had exacted. Everyone noticed their heavily bloodsoaked clothing but decided it was the blood of the victims of the massacre. They were also painfully aware of a flight of media correspondents flying up from Saigon once the story was released. It was common knowledge that the liberal press was increasingly pacifist. They would turn every angle to demonize the military for waging an unjust war against the Vietnamese people.

It was early Monday morning when Jim Tate arrived at the Castle, rapping on its door as well as that of the Shanty. Richard and Fritz were annoyed as they had left Betty's shortly before dawn as Poker Night ended. Some of the highlights of the night came when it was announced that the big winners would be playing for a piece of Loki's ass. The players howled with laughter when she punched more than one of the men in the face as hard as she could as the evening progressed.

"C'mon, Jim, what the hell are you doing up this early?" Richard whined as Fritz came out without the usual cups of coffee.

"Hey, it's not like I stopped off for breakfast," Jim retorted. "Fred wants a word."

They trudged down the path behind Jim as errant schoolboys on the way to the principal's office. They plopped down into seats in front of Captain Federer's desk. There was already a cloud of cigar smoke over his head as he was puffing in a pique. He pulled a small deck of large photos from a folder and tossed it across the desk before them.

"Are these for a movie?" Fritz said lamely. "Not very realistic."

"*Fick nicht mit mir,*" Federer blazed.

"*Ich habe nicht gesagt,*" Fritz was defensive.

"What are they saying?" Richard asked Jim.

"Hell if I know."

Richard took a second look at the black and white photos of ten severed pelvises impaled upon poles in a row on a jungle clearing. They were positioned so that the buttocks could be seen wedged upon the poles.

"The boys from Airmobile happened to be running recon in the area and flew down to investigate," Fred settled down somewhat. "You know how they like to take pictures. Unfortunately they brought them back to Saigon and it fell into the hands of the regular Army. They came up and took some souvenir shots."

"Looks like Charlie had a big falling out," Richard mused.

"I told you guys I was under the glass here," Fred was reignited. "Luckily the Colonel realized the enemy must have been watching the village before the attack. This crap here --- this is inexplicable. Why didn't you report the altercation? And what in hell gave you the idea to do something like this?"

"C'mon, Fred," Fritz reasoned. "You weren't there. The Marines only took pictures of the body bags. You saw the reports. It was an atrocity. We gave them a receipt."

"Let me explain something to you guys," Fred looked over his bifocals at them. "We got the media crawling around Saigon like cockroaches. The liberals are plastering anti-war propaganda all over the Western World. When they're not showing our boys in the hospital, they're taking pictures of burning villages. They got pictures of naked kids running down streets in *Time Magazine*. What do you think they'll do with stuff like this?"

"So why isn't MACV publicizing Charlie's stuff?" Richard wondered.

"MACV isn't in the news business," Fred was insistent. "Plus there's things the assholes in Geneva might consider war crimes, at the least. Did you ever consider the fact that a rational person might see this and recommend you guys for a Section Eight?"

"Okay, point taken," Richard conceded. "We weren't planning on our boys giving us up. We figured Charlie would come over to see why their butchers didn't come back. The Vietnamese have a thing about planting their dead so their spirits don't roam the earth. We figured they'd be underground before something like this happened."

"G'wan, get lost," Fred put the photos back in the folder. "I'm gonna have to write a report about an inch thick to make this go away. Jim, talk to them."

"Will do," Jim replied.

"So what, you gonna read us the riot act?" Richard ribbed him as they left the office.

"Not really," he cocked an eyebrow. "Let me explain something to you. Remember when you were in grade school and the classroom bully got in your face during recess? The day came when you finally laid him out, but you both got taken to the principal's office even though you were in the right."

"I went to Catholic school," Richard smirked. "The nuns would drag you into the hallway and throw a beating on you."

"Same here," Fritz guffawed as they slapped palms.

"Here's the thing," Jim confided. "I'm sure there was a time when you ran into the bully in the street or somewhere when no one was around. You kicked his ass, and no one ever found out about it. I know because we would've never known you messed Charlie up if those pics hadn't turned up."

"Yeah, there's always a downside," Richard agreed. "I would've added to my registered kills if we could've called it in."

"If we could've figured which kill was which," Fritz snickered.

"The point I'm making is that if nobody sees it, it never happened." Jim was emphatic. "I know the big thing with MACV and the Pentagon is the count. The more kills we report, the better we look on paper. That's fine until we get sent out on recon or get these special missions where we end up in a bloodbath. That's where we got to use common sense. Everybody wants to bump their kill score. But what you don't want is the stuff in Fred's folder. What you don't want is your name on Westmoreland's desk. And most of all, you never want to take a one-way trip to Leavenworth."

"Gotcha, Chief," Richard nodded.

"Well, I'm off," Jim yawned as he took his leave. "I've got a hunting trip planned with the warriors in the morning. We'll probably spend the day doing all kinds of stuff that never happened."

3

THE JUDAS TREE

Richard rose earlier than usual this morning, having set his alarm for a half hour before sunrise. He would be skipping his routine morning coffee with Fritz, which he would explain later in the day. He decided that he would start this day with a long overdue visit with Grandpa.

Only Fritz dared call Jim Tate Grandpa to his face. The rest of the team affably called him Chief. He was Captain Federer's liaison with the team and, together with Fritz, was their main connection to the Montagnard mountain dwellers. He reported to Fred daily and kept a short-wave radio in his cabin for emergencies. He met with the team as needed, but remained at the Nest other than to go out hunting with the Warriors.

Richard admired the view as he took Path One down the Valley to where it took a dogleg onto an uphill road. It overlooked the Minefield, which was the size of a football field stretching one hundred yards toward the DMZ (*Demilitarized Zone) and the North Vietnam border. It featured rows upon rows of concertina wire which was sprinkled liberally with tripwires and landmines. There was a map at HQ showing where the mines were located, but no one of sound mind would go out to check.

The Minefield was often a cause for celebration at the camp and the mountain village. When an explosion was heard, the warriors would come down to investigate. Sometimes it was an NVA (*North Vietnamese Army) sniper sent on a suicide mission. At other times it was a VC team acting out of ignorance. The most joyous occasion came when an ox or cattle happened to stray. It would be blown apart, and the warriors would retrieve the carcass and bring it back to the village for a feast.

Richard saw two armed guards when he arrived at the cabin, and they made themselves scarce as he knocked on the doorframe.

"Enter."

Richard adjusted his vision to the candlelit room, where Jim sat crosslegged before an altar extending across the back wall. At the center was a golden statue of Xo, the Montagnard deity. On either side were what Richard recognized as totem poles. They exchanged greetings before Richard crossed his legs and took a seat.

"Looks like you've gone all in with the Yards," Richard nodded at Xo.

"The Cherokee believe that the Great Spirit manifests himself to all people in different ways," Jim glanced at the triple-headed statue. "The Bru believe that the heads represent truth, liberty and justice. It's refreshing to know that it is what our American flag stands for. In that we agree."

"My Mom's grandfather was part Cheyenne," Richard disclosed. "I've been thinking a lot about him lately. I was brought up Southern Baptist. We are aware of the existence of evil spirits and demons. I've felt them ever since I arrived In-

Country. As the hippies might say, there's lots of bad vibes around these parts."

"We believe there is medicine for body and soul," Jim nodded to a long ceremonial token on the small table between them. "Would you care to partake of the pipe of peace?"

"Sure, I'm game."

Jim lit the pipe and took a long drag before handing it to his guest. The stem was two feet long, its bowl resembling the head of a serpent. Richard took a drag and did his best to avoid coughing up the powerful smoke.

"It is a sacred herb only grown in the mountain villages," Jim told him. "Its legend has grown over the centuries. In days of old, the Vietnamese, Cambodians, Laotians and Chinese tribes launched campaigns to subdue the mountain folk and take what was theirs. Very often they came in search of the sacred herb. To this day, the lowlanders have never achieved their quest."

"This is some strong shit," Richard handed the pipe back. Within minutes it seemed as if everything in the room was surrounded by a neon-tinged aura. He glanced at his hand and it had become as phosphorescent. "I can see why the gooks would come up here trying to rip them off."

"Some times it was for the herb," Jim mused. "Other times it was a search for truth. Christians believe the Great Spirit had a Son Who came to Earth to bring the Truth to men. He was rejected by men, and despite His efforts they turned on Him out of fear and ignorance. He was tried, convicted and killed. During his trial, the evil rulers asked Him, 'What is Truth?'. As we know, some men cannot recognize Truth when it stands before their eyes."

"Since we're in a trippy mood, let's go back to what we were discussing the other day," Richard struggled to focus. "You were going on about how if you don't see it, it didn't happen.

I've heard lots of stories about you and the Warriors going out and getting in some major shootouts. How do you fellows make it not happen?"

"There is a Tree of Knowledge of Good and Evil at the end of the winding road," Jim replied. "I believe the spirit of your ancestor sent you here this morning. I think this is part of your vision quest. Outside you will find the trail, and you can see for yourself."

Richard managed to regain his feet and make it back out into the brilliant sunrise. He slung his AK-47 over his shoulder and saw a warrior motion toward his right. He saw a gravel path marked by a sycamore tree leading down a slope due northwest. He took a deep breath and headed down the road that led through a wooded area.

The first thing he noticed was the smell. It reeked of the dead, and he had to breathe through his mouth to keep from choking. There was enough of the residue from the peace pipe in his lungs to make it not entirely unpleasant. Only the path grew narrower, and he found himself treading on a mushy topsoil that reminded him of the dream he had the other night. When it looked down he saw a rubbery consistency that resembled blood pudding.

He looked up and beheld the ugliest tree he had ever seen. Its trunk was thirty feet tall and wide, the knots on its bulging center appearing as the eyes, nose and mouth of an idol. Its limbs and branches seemed as arms and hands outstretched toward the skies in agony. There was a horrid sap leaking from cracks in the trunk that resembled the rotten entrails of corpses.

He inched closer and could see there were pieces of bone protruding from the ground, as if the earth regurgitated what it could no longer bear. Suddenly it dawned on him that this was where the Warriors buried that which they did not want to matter. All the evidence of their blood feuds, tribal wars and military campaigns were laid to rest here, this hideous tree sworn to its secrecy.

"Are you Indian?"

Richard was startled and nearly raised his weapon as he whirled to face the warrior behind him.

"Yeah, so I've been told."

"We thought so," the diminutive man said, three of his fellow hunters appearing at his back. Like the Crazy Eight, they wore only loincloths and boots, carrying bow and arrows. "Jim asked us to accompany you on our hunting trip in his stead."

"Sounds good to me. I'm not overly familiar with the area, so you lead the way."

He knew they were about ten miles east of Cam Lo, which made him comfortable heading in that direction. At length they came to within sight of Route 16 which connected Dong Ha to Cam Lo. Richard told the warriors they would move through the woods about thirty yards from the road so they could not be seen. They continued westward, looking for signs of anything unusual that would be worth checking out.

Their expectations were met as they noticed commotion a few yards from the highway. There was a chattering of monkeys that might have indicated the presence of a beast of prey. Richard signaled them left and right as he crept in to investigate. He spotted the monkeys in a tall tree hurling nuts down at an interloper. In turn they were pelted by a barrage of rocks which forced them to flee from their perches.

"Hurry it up, will you?" a rifleman snapped at his confederate, who was furtively working beneath the hood of a steaming delivery truck. "We're way behind schedule."

"I need to pour in the antifreeze, you fool," they bantered back and forth in Vietnamese. "You want the damned thing to blow up?"

"You call him a fool and you're pouring antifreeze in the jungle?" a third rifleman smoked a cigarette as he leaned against the back of the truck.

"Keep your mouth closed," the mechanic retorted. "You're about as smart as your relatives you just threw rocks at."

"You continue making noise and the damned Marines will be here before you know it," the fourth man shook himself after taking a leak in the bushes.

"The Marines are going to be the least of your problems," a voice called out in a Missourian accent.

The VC smugglers had no time to react as a hail of automatic fire was sprayed in their direction. The mechanic jerked wildly, bumping against the prop rod so that the hood dropped on his head. The rifleman alongside him danced as a marionette before collapsing to the ground. The guerrilla near the rear bumper lifted his rifle as an arrow pierced his right eyeball and emerged from the back of his skull. Richard walked up to the wounded man by the bushes and blew his brains out as canned spaghetti with a shotgun blast.

"Let's see what they were hauling here," Richard ordered. "Y Wop, make sure that brute finished pouring the antifreeze so we can roll out of here."

The warrior was unsure as to the name given him, but nodded as he checked the fluid level. His cousin was far more exultant as he beckoned to Richard.

"Damn, you fellows brought me some luck," he crowed as he pried one of the crates open. There were a dozen AK-47 Kalashnikov rifles in a dozen crates along with smaller crates which contained ammunition magazines. The Russian-made automatic rifles were arguably superior to their American-made Armalite counterparts in that they rarely jammed and were considered weatherproof in their ability to fire after being dropped in mud or water. The VC greatly preferred them to the Chinese-made Type 56 rifle that the NVA routinely supplied.

"Let us surprise the Lieutenant with them," Wop was delighted. "He will be well pleased."

"Lieutenant, my ass," Richard scoffed. "We're driving these to Saigon. I just met a fellow who might pay us serious money for this. You guys'll be able to buy a truckload of bananas for each of your families."

And so they continued along Route 16, two of the warriors in back while Richard drove with Wop as co-pilot. It was an old Sixties truck, and it took a while before he got reacquainted with the standard clutch pedal and gear shift. His experience as a Missourian farm boy shone through, and soon they were cruising along at 60 MPH. He planned on taking QL 14 between Krong Klang and Tan Hop which would set them on course to Saigon due north.

They were hindered by the appearance of a cobra in the road. Richard ran over it, only to see it writhing in agony in the rear view mirror. He stopped the truck and got out, walking back to chop its head off.

"You stopped to put a snake out of its misery?" Wop marveled, thinking that he was in the presence of a highly spiritual man.

"Now, you can't help being a Montagnard, right?" Richard gunned the engine as they continued along. "Well, he couldn't help being a snake."

The remark changed Wop's opinion of the Missourian as they sailed down the road. Only Richard was perplexed as to how a cobra found its way onto the highway. His concern heightened as they drove a couple of miles to find a thick tree limb blocking the road.

"Hey, you two," Richard banged on the back panel. "Get that shit out of the way."

The warriors clambered out of the back and trotted over to the debris. They stopped short at the sight of two camouflage-clad riflemen springing out from the treeline and moving in front of the limb. Richard spotted movement in the rear view mirror and saw four riflemen scurrying onto the road behind them.

"Stand down, Y Crud," Richard vaulted out of the truck. The warrior, puzzled by his new name, reluctantly set his long knife down on the pavement.

"Reckon you just saved that little bastard's life," a hulking man with a red mane and a Fu Manchu mustache drawled with a Texas accent.

"Thank you for your service," Richard was sarcastic. "Now get that shit out of my way so I can get out of yours."

"Whatcha toting there, pardner?"

"Swag. I aim to run it down to Saigon for a fair price."

"There's laws against that, fellow. Wanna end up in Leavenworth?"

"I'm with Special Forces at Dong Ha. Who in hell are you?"

"You're in Lurp territory. We're on the lookout for slopes wanting for payback after what you fellows pulled out your way a few days ago. Hung their asses out to dry, they say. Nice touch."

"Yeah, well, we'll take our chances."

"That's a no can do. Word's out that the Red Khmer (*Khmer Rouge) may be coming in force from across the border. You get diced and sliced, we'd be responsible."

"Guess we got a Mexican standoff. I'm not giving this score up. I'm Green Beret Mafia, you should know that."

"Look, I can handle this for you," he reasoned. "I'm Big Tex, I'm known in Saigon. I report directly to Buffalo Bill."

"Keep talking."

"I'll take your basics and have my guys run this downtown for you. I get a ten percent service charge, but you can consider that a life insurance payment. I split my end twelve ways, just so you know. We get the goods to Bill, he deposits for you. If anything goes sideways, Bill compensates fifty percent of the verified loss."

"And if it goes missing and Bill finds out, he takes your balls off."

"Something like that."

Richard came by the Castle for coffee and was invited inside by Fritz. They agreed as they both mentioned they had something to discuss. Once they were seated, Richard gave a detailed account of what had transpired the previous day.

"I was hoping you may be able to check on the transaction for me," Richard concluded. "Or at least provide some guidance. It's not so much about the money. I just want to make sure I wasn't ripped off and that I'm not being disrespected."

"Things were pretty momentous here as well," Fritz revealed. "I had a visitor from the Company (*CIA). Quite informative. It wasn't as much a proposition as it was a glimpse into the future."

"Pray tell."

"It seems that they're muscling in on the Golden Triangle network. We know that the bulk of the VC's financing comes from the drug trade. Pure heroin is funneled in from Thailand, Laos and Burma, none of which are involved in this conflict. It gets shipped along the Ruak and Mekong Rivers and smuggled across the globe."

"You memorize all that?"

"Yeah, sort of. Anyway, when it shows up on the Ho Chi Minh Trail it's fair game. The Company's been taking steps to intercept it before it crosses into Vietnam. Once it's here, though, it's a problem. Most of it gets shipped to America. We know President Johnson's moving on and Richard Nixon may win the election in September. If he does, he'll be stepping down hard on that anti-drug plank in his platform. That means the drug traffickers are going into overdrive to move as much dope as they can before then."

"So how does that affect us?"

"The Company's paying top dollar for intercepted shipments. Buffalo Bill gets twenty percent for moving swag. The Company's buying it at the going rate, no percentage."

"I got a problem," Richard exhaled. "It's no reflection or judgment on you. It's just that I'm a Southern Baptist, it's part of who I am. I don't mind confiscating stolen goods and taking a cut for turning it over to whoever. I just can't have anything to do with drugs. If I take it from Charlie, it's gotta burn. It's my way."

"Okay," Fritz relented. "There's a lot of money in the drug trade, but I didn't earn my green beanie for money. Neither did you. I'm about the body count, and so are you. The swag is icing on the cake. And MACV is a lot less likely to burn our tails over guns, alcohol or tobacco than drugs."

He reached across the coffee table and they shook hands.

"I like you, Richard. You're like a brother I never met."

"Same here. I think you know that."

"We can do a helluva lot of good here, you and me and Grandpa. I'll let the agents know that we'll turn any drugs we grab over to them at no charge. I'm sure they'll be delighted. On the upside, I'm sure they'll owe us some favors that may come in handy."

They let it go at that and planned to meet at Betty's that evening for some R&R (*rest and recreation) with the Team. The relationship was gradually improving as the Team was developing a greater respect for the teammates manning the outposts. The active patrolling by Jim and Fritz's Montagnard units were enhancing the profile of the camp. The VC and the NVA knew of its reputation and were treading lightly in the area. Although they initially considered Jim, Fritz and Richard standoffish, they were coming to a deeper respect for the contributions the threesome was making.

Betty's was hopping as usual. Jerry Brown was running his card game in the back area with George Bullski along with Bostonite Sean O'Bannon and Brooklynites Chuck Valentine and Al Last. They laughed and joked boisterously between hands and yelled and cursed at the end of each game. Luke Sanderson, a Kentuckian, had a moonshine still and enjoyed smoking weed on occasion. He greatly enjoyed stepping outside with Jim Tate and sharing a joint along the course of the evening.

"Who's that fellow?" Richard motioned to a small, clean-shaven, compact man sitting alone with a bottle in a far corner.

"That's Bobby Cuddahy," Fritz replied. "We think he's got a stress disorder, but he won't ship out. He won't talk to anyone except Fred and that's when he's called to the office. He's lucky Jim's the looie (*lieutenant). Jim goes into spiritual mode and asks him yes and no questions when they need to go over things. All he does is nod."

"Well, I'd like to meet him."

Cuddahy had the million-mile stare of the traumatized vet. Only when Richard gazed into his eyes it was as the bottomless pit. This man had lost his soul in the vortex.

"You know who Richard Mc Cain is," Fritz introduced them "I told him you were a very capable man and a man of honor. Richard is Green Beret Mafia, he's one of us. I know that you can rely on each other for anything you might need."

They shook hands, and Cuddahy poured shot glasses for his guests. He kept twelve shot glasses at his table along with a quart of Jack Daniels whiskey. Richard and Fritz touched glasses with him and downed their shots before taking their leave.

"He's got a cold fish handshake," Richard noted as they left the saloon.

"It's something they do at the asylums back in the World," Fritz explained. "It means they'll slit your throat without skipping a beat. You always want a guy like that at your side, but never at your back."

A couple of days later, Richard showed up at The Castle at daybreak with concerns. They retreated inside so Fritz could get the lowdown.

"I checked my Swiss account and found out I only got five grand," Richard informed him. "I should've gotten ten. That Big Tex jarhead burned me."

"Son of a bitch," Fritz grunted. "How do you want to handle this?"

"If I call him to a sitdown he won't pay up, I'm pretty sure of it. He's the kind of guy who'll say the shipment was short. He'll know we didn't open each crate and check the load. My word against his."

"If we call him out and he doesn't back down, we'll have a beef with the Lurps, which isn't good," Fritz mused. "You wanna pass on this one?"

"If I do that he'll think I'm weak, and he'll spread the word, Look, set up a sitdown with Bill for tomorrow night."

"Let me check my schedule," Fritz suggested. "I told Fred

I'd check the northwest sector along the Minefield tomorrow night. We're thinking Charlie's been snooping around out there. Maybe we can go Thursday."

"No, go on and set it up. I'll go out with Bobby Cuddahy."

Traffic was frenetic as usual at Saigon on Thursday night. They caught a cargo flight from Dong Ha Combat Base to Saigon and took a cab to the warehouse along the outskirts of the downtown area. The driver darted through traffic and barely missed hitting a rickshaw before they reached their destination. Richard glanced over at Bobby, whose demeanor never changed. He appeared as if he was watching a boring TV show. Their attire was just as discrepant, with Richard wearing a $200 blue silk suit with matching tie and patent leather boots. Bobby wore a black suit and tie that seemed as if acquired at a thrift store.

Once again they had to go through security, and the commandos were cleared by two riflemen carrying a walkie talkie. They entered the cavernous warehouse and crossed the floor to where Buffalo Bill sat at an enormous desk. On his right hand side sat a smug-looking Big Tex. They, unlike their counterparts, were dressed in field camouflage and green T-shirts.

"Sgt. Hammer explained the situation when he called to set up the meet," Bill opened the discussion as Richard and Bobby took their seats on the left side of the desk. "I discussed it with Tex, and he told me his story. I'm sure you want to go over it again."

"I ripped off a VC smuggling crew while I was out on recon, " Richard said flatly. "Your associate here had a toll road set up. We came across a cobra they had set out as sign. Naturally we couldn't read it, so we got stopped. He told me he'd move the load here for ten percent. Turns out the son of a bitch took half."

"Better watch your mouth, beanie boy," Big Tex snarled. "This is gyrene territory."

"The only reason why I didn't come for you is because I didn't want to mess up any arrangement," Richard glared at him. "It's the only reason why you're sitting here in one piece."

"All right, let's settle down," Bill held up a hand before Tex could respond. "They took the count and said the crates were half full. They said they paid what they counted."

"The guys I put down were hardcore VC," Richard flushed angrily. "They were moving south from Quang Tri Province, which means it came through the DMZ. There's no frigging way they got shorted by the NVA. Plus I didn't need his blessing in the first place. If I knew this was gonna happen, I would've driven through without a problem."

"Oh, you would've had a problem, all right," Tex was belligerent.

"No, you got a problem," Richard narrowed his eyes.

With that, Bobby Cuddahy stood up and drew a .22 pistol, shooting Tex in the left thigh. He screamed in pain as the riflemen rushed across the floor.

"Get him out of here," Bill ordered as they came to Tex's side and hoisted him on their shoulders, pulling him away.

Bill stared at Bobby and was as fascinated by the soulless gaze as was Richard upon their meeting.

"Okay, how do we fix this?

"I want my money," Richard insisted. "I don't give a damn about the amount, it's a matter of principle. You should know that. You make me whole, then it's between you and him. Look, this is a drop in the bucket compared to what's ahead."

"What's ahead is that shithead peacenik Nixon coming in with his War on Drugs bullshit," Bill fumed. "We're having an

End of Season clearance sale. If he wins in September, he won't get sworn in until January. That gives us just enough time to make sure we don't leave anything on the table."

"Look, my partner Fritz and I aren't moving drugs, so that's out."

"Then what's your angle?"

"ATF," Richard grinned slyly. "Alcohol, tobacco and firearms. Let's reason together. Charlie runs muscle for a criminal empire stretching across Vietnam. The government's in on it, the underworld's directing traffic and they're bleeding the country dry. Look, I believe in the Cause. I fight for God and country. I hate the nabobs as bad as I hate Charlie. I believe the black market is the people's market. If we can rob Charlie of what he steals, we can get it to your network and the people can buy it for half of what the government sells it for."

"Well, that's one way of looking at it," Bill frowned. "I like to think we're part of the greater good when I go to bed at night, even though when all is said and done I don't give a shit. Hey, we're not going to change this country any more than the French did before Charlie ran them off. We're not gonna get them to quit drinking or smoking, or shooting dope, any more than we can get them to stop eating rice and fish sauce. I just don't see Charlie making the profit. As far as the guns, that goes to the militia, which is how it should be. Why should a village be taxed for government arms when I can send them a box of Armalites for the cost of their dumb ox?"

"I'm glad we see things eye to eye," Richard nodded. "Here's the plan. I'm gonna put my own team of Yards together and start patrolling the northeast sector. Fritz has been hitting the southeast and Jim Tate's stomping the southeast. You jarheads are doing a decent job along the southwest. We got all bases covered. The only way Charlie will be able to move their cargo is along the Ho Chi Minh Trail, which is currently being bombed to hell by the Air Force. He'll have to make some stupid moves somewhere, and that's where we'll make our big scores."

"The only way he can move is along the seacoast," Bill mused. "That puts him up against the Vietnamese Navy and the Coast Guard. Definitely not a safe place."

"That's why I'm looking forward to working the northeast sector," Richard smiled. "Charlie will be playing the coast the way they've been moving along the Cambodian border. Every time they get into shit with the jarheads, they run out of bounds at the border so you can't chase them down. I'm thinking they're gonna start playing the same game along the shore. I want to set up a play where I can give Charlie enough rope to hang himself. And you and I will be the major benefactors."

"I did some research on your ass after you came by with Hammer," Bill was frank. "You did yourself proud in II Corps, especially during Tet. One hundred eight registered kills, and this is only your first year In Country. Plus you picked up a silver star and a bronze. You are definitely Born Again. Now, I don't like what you and your fish-eyed friend did to my man here. Only I figure he had it coming."

"A man lives and dies by his rep here," Richard said firmly. "I respect you just as I demand respect."

Bill reached into a drawer and pulled out five rolls of $100 bills which he set across the desk. Richard wordlessly put them in his pockets.

"Okay," Bill stood up and shook hands with his guests. "We have an understanding and an agreement. Fritz Hammer's your middleman. Any problems, you go to Hammer and he reaches out to me."

Richard felt optimistic as they caught a cab and headed back to the air base.

There was money in the air. He could smell it.

4

WALKING DEAD

"This is a war that the white man has waged against us since World War II," the speaker held his small audience spellbound. "Be not deceived, we have fought for our freedom since the beginning of time. All of the surrounding nations --- the Cambodians, the Laotians, the Chinese, the Japanese, even the Montagnards have tried to subjugate our people and enslave our country. Yet we have endured. And we will continue to endure. Just as we chased the French as dogs from our land, so shall we cause the Americans to flee as herds of swine. But we must face facts, my brothers. This is a larger and more powerful enemy than the French. This is a monstrous giant we face. Yet we will emerge victorious."

"Not only do they rape our land and steal our resources. They send our young men to slaughter and poison the minds of our children. They sell our women into whoredom and turn our elderly into beggars in the dust. Their mission is to contradict and ridicule our beliefs, our traditions, our society and culture. They despise the Father of our Country, Ho Chi Minh, as an illegitimate ruler and an insurrectionist. They seek to replace the popular economy of socialism with their perverted and exploitative system of capitalism. The Republicans are the puppets of the white devils, and they will face justice when the Americans are vanquished once and forever."

The speaker was of unpleasant appearance, many calling him the Josef Goebbels of North Vietnam. He had a head resembling that of a praying mantis. At the peak of his sloped head was a meticulously coiffed black pompadour which was so heavily greased as to seem as a plastic mold. He had beady eyes which many compared to those of a serpent. Beneath this was a pug nose and a cruel mouth. When he spoke he raised his upper lip so as to seem all the more vicious. His cheeks were covered with pock marks and acne scars making him most repulsive.

This man was Michael "Chink" Abesamis.

"He's one ugly bastard, I'll grant you that," Fritz Hammer said as he tossed the photos on the conference table before him.

"Army Intelligence has an extensive dossier on this guy," Captain Federer strode behind the table where Fritz sat along with the rest of the A Team at the meeting that Monday morning. "We think he's an agent for the Ministry of State Security in China. He reports directly to Ho Chi Minh and General Giap. The VC sends their agents into unstable villages to do the research. When they find out who the leaders are and the causes of their discontent, they go to work. They pin the blame on the government and provide quick fixes where possible. If that doesn't work they resort to kidnapping and murder. Once the village chiefs capitulate, the Chink moves in. He reprograms the village leaders, and now the village belongs to Charlie."

"And that's how our Army patrols get ambushed," Richard frowned. "Then when they send in the Marines to burn the village down, the media comes in and accuses us of war crimes."

"Yep, a win-win for Charlie," Fred agreed. "It's like a cancer. When we relocate the villagers, Charlie's undercover agents go right along with them. We help them build a fortified hamlet somewhere, and we may just as well be setting up a new shop for Victor Charles."

"So what's our play?" Jerry Brown asked.

"I'll have the ARVN plaster this guy's face all over the surrounding hamlets," Fred replied. "We'll offer a hundred dong (*Vietnamese dollar) for his capture."

"Gee, Fred, that's not even one cent," Steve Korn raised an eyebrow.

"Okay, a hundred thousand," Fred huffed.

"That's about four bucks, skipper," Jerry ribbed him.

"A hundred bucks American, you figure it out," Fred snorted. "Here's the deal. Thanks to Jim and Fritz, with kudos to our new friend Richard, our friends up North are getting annoyed by our hunting trips. Especially over the asses-on-poles episode a few days ago that almost got us on the front page of *Time* Magazine thanks to I-Wonder-Who."

The room was filled with hoots and catcalls accentuated by fist and palm thumps on the table.

"Okay, knock it off," Fred growled. "Our friends at the Company have given Army Intel a tip-off that the NVA themselves may be paying us a visit. They're looking to test the Minefield to see if they can neutralize it for a major end run. Obviously they'll be risking a major loss up front, but if they detonate enough mines in the process, we may not be able to replace them for a follow-up run."

"Smart move," Luke Sanderson nodded. "Most likely they'll send old Victor Charlie in first to blow them mines. If they pull back before dawn, they know we'll use the daylight to do the patchwork. They can get some high-faluting video equipment out to see how and where our dinks replace everything."

"I'd volunteer for damage control," Richard replied. "I'd use smoke screens and mine-drops by helicopter. Plus I'm sure me and Jim could think up some nasty new traps. But I'm with Fred. We need to pay visits to our outposts and make sure Charlie hasn't stolen all those hearts and minds we worked so hard to win."

The meeting was adjourned shortly thereafter, and Richard and Fritz headed back down Path Five to the clearing. Upon arrival they spotted an exotic bottle to which was taped a small envelope. Fritz opened the card and handed the bottle to Richard.

"It's written in Gook," Fritz smirked. "I think it says Thank You, I may be wrong."

"I've had some of this before," Richard uncorked the bottle and smelled the aroma. "This is Ruoude, it's dink moonshine. Do this up on an off day and it can put you on your ass."

"Well, it's Team patrol day," Fritz crossed the drawbridge and opened the Castle door. "I think Chuck and Al are going out. They'll probably be handing out pics of that ugly Chink *hurensohn* (*son of a bitch)."

"It's gonna create a lot of confusion. The slopes'll be thinking Thang Co Hon (*Vietnamese Halloween) arrived early."

They shared a laugh before Fritz went around lighting candles and setting out glasses. Richard sat down and tossed the cap of the bottle away, pouring shots for them. Missourians did so in tradition, indicating they would empty the contents and that none would get so tipsy as to knock over the bottle and spill a drop.

They proceeded to empty the bottle over hours of

fellowship, and Richard never realized at what point he fell into a long sleep.

It was briefly interrupted by hands grabbing at him and lifting him. He tried to fight back but was reassured that he would be taken care of. He tried to focus but the effects of the liquor was far too powerful, and he passed out once again.

After an eternity he shook his head and cleared the cobwebs. It reminded him of his visit to Jim's cabin. He was so foggy that it almost seemed as if he was dreaming. Yet he saw Fritz outside in the clearing and joined him. Night had fallen beneath a starry sky.

"I heard everybody's leaving," Fritz said quietly. "I figured we'd stay behind."

"Well, thanks for asking," Richard replied sarcastically.

Richard and Fritz watched dourly as the small caravan of trucks left the compound via the rear exit. They waited until the taillights of the last vehicle disappeared along the road before securing the armored gate. Among the evacuees were the LLDB, the Vietnamese and Montagnard irregulars, and the camp followers who resided by the compound. They could see the Marines were placed in charge of the move and were probably moving everything to Dong Ha Combat Base.

"Damned jarheads," Richard grumbled. "Took everything with them."

"Stands to reason," Fritz frowned. "If we get overrun, Charlie won't have anything left to play with."

The Lurps arrived in confirmation of I Corps' command to abandon the Green Berets' Dong Ha compound in anticipation of the scheduled air strike. Captain Federer had petitioned General Westmoreland but was denied permission to hold the fort. He was greatly reluctant to leave Hammer and Mc Cain behind, but the commandos were insistent to the verge of insubordination.

Or so Richard could vaguely recall.

"Okay," he said before leaving the camp. "It's your funeral."

They settled along the northern compound wall until 0300 as scheduled. They were as kids hiding in the shadows awaiting Halloween. At once they were astounded by a firestorm that was as a nuclear explosion engulfing the entire minefield beyond the concertina-lined outer perimeter. The heat was so intense that they both fell backwards, feeling their heads to see if their hair had been singed.

Do us proud. Do us proud.

"I got film in my eyes," Richard rolled to his side, wiping his eyes.

"It's eyeball tissue," Fritz managed a chuckle. "A day's worth of desert march."

They returned to their positions, their lungs filled with the smell of napalm as the Phantom jets streaked away. They had trouble readjusting their vision from the blinding light of the strike. Eventually they could discern explosions beyond the concertina as an incalculable mass of humanity pressed forth inexorably from the shadows.

"It's gotta be a division," Richard marveled. "How can they keep coming through all that?"

They came to realize that the two divisions (North Vietnamese Army and Viet Cong) had been struck by napalm. Most of the survivors forged ahead on muscle memory though they were clinically brain dead. The forward units were disintegrated by the land mines as the next wave swept forth and became entangled in the razor wire. Those behind them continued to surge, trampling their comrades before they were mashed against the fenceline.

"They're coming through," Fritz grabbed his rifle as the

tandem retreated toward the barracks area. "I don't think we should waste ammo. They're so messed up, we can probably take them out with close combat weapons."

"Not like the Marines left us much to choose from," Richard grunted. "Say, how about those baseball bats we got from Saigon last week?"

They raced into the barracks and retrieved the Louisville sluggers they had ordered. Both men had played high school baseball and were considered quality home run hitters. They saw the enemy flattening the fenceline and rushed to its defense.

The enemy were as zombies, charred black from head to boots and sandals. They shuffled forth as mummies, their bayoneted rifles held diagonally as if in parade formation. At first the Americans took leaps and bounds in swinging their bats. The force of the blows snapped the enemies' necks like twigs, sending their heads flying through the air. Soon the men settled down and began decapitating the enemy with measured swipes.

"Ow!" Fritz hissed as Richard turned to see where a VC bayonet sliced a gash across his forearm. "That asshole took a swipe at me."

"They got me too," he pointed to a bleeding wound across his torso. "I think the ones in the rear are still functional."

"I only have a couple of magazines," Fritz groped his cargo pants pockets. "Not enough to finish them off. Looks like there's at least a couple of platoons left."

"How about those tractors we got last week?"

"Now that's thinking on your feet," Fritz chuckled.

The men raced to the shed behind the barracks and climbed into the seats of the tractors sent from Saigon. They gunned the engines and steered the farm vehicles out from behind the barracks. The tractors headed straight for the herd, their plows and treads grinding the enemy into cinders.

After over a half hour's work, the chore finally ended. Richard Mc Cain was an experienced farmhand from his youth in Missouri, as was Fritz Hammer from his childhood in North Dakota. They were able to dig shallow trenches and neatly shovel the remnants of the zombies away.

"Well, that's a hard day's night," Richard joined Fritz outside the barracks as they surveyed their work. "I've got a bottle of Jack Daniels inside."

"I got Courvoisier," Fritz replied.

"Let's have at it."

The two friends retreated to the lounge area and drank until sunrise. They then retired to a well-deserved rest.

Richard woke from a dreamless sleep and saw a Bru shaman beating a small drum above him as he muttered arcane chants. There were two stands where incense smoldered at the head and foot of the cot where he laid.

"Well, well, look who's back," Al Last, the Team medical specialist, rushed bedside as Richard shooed the shaman away.

"How the hell did I get here?"

"Long story short, you and Fritz drank enough strychnine to kill a horse," Al informed him. "That bottle of Ruoude was poisoned, not so much that you'd detect it."

"Damn," Richard rose to a sitting position, realizing he was in the Team barracks at Deadwood. "There was an air strike scheduled around these parts, wasn't there?"

"Yep, you and Fritz slept right through it."

"Well, hell's bells," Richard pulled his T-shirt, fatigues and boots back on. "Where is he now?"

"He left about a half hour ago, Guess he drank less than

you did. One of his Crazy Eight boys came up, said they had a lead on the guy who left the bottle. Say, where you going? I need to check you out before you head out."

"I'll get with you later," Richard headed out the door. "Don't wanna miss out on all the fun."

Richard arrived at the Castle and was motioned to enter by Y Bro and Y Den, who stood guard outside. He went in and beheld an elderly man tied and blindfolded in a chair in the middle of the room, the chair standing in a child's wading pool. He was soaking wet, and Fritz had a kettle on a hot plate set atop a nearby table.

"Time for tea?" Richard smiled tautly.

"He's had some already, but you can have whatever you like," Fritz replied airily. "I told him I'll continue pouring half the kettle on his head and refilling it until he talks. It's been warming gradually, but when it starts to boil I think his mood might change."

"And what's his story?"

"Y Pes thinks Charlie got to him in leaving us that wonderful little bottle of moonshine."

"Is that so?"

Richard pulled his Bowie knife and swiftly sliced through the duct tape that bound his wrists and ankles. He grabbed the old man and slung him to the floor, then mounted his back and applied a crossface submission hold. The victim screamed as he tapped out and was released as Y Pes came out from the shadows to hear his confession. The man was babbling too quickly for the Americans to understand.

"The VC knew he comes up here to cut the grass weekly," Y Pes explained. "They threatened his wife and children if he did not leave the bottle. They are from the coast, they are the

Green River Killers. They said that all those who live along the coast are loyal to Ho Chi Minh. All who do not comply with them will be slaughtered on the day of reckoning."

"Looks like that day just came and went," Richard smirked. "Payback Day is just around the corner."

"Take him down to Deadwood and have him and his family checked out," Fritz pulled a $100 bill from his wallet. "Tell Fred we want them sent to IV Corps for resettlement. Witness Protection Program, or whatever. And tell him if I ever see him again I'll kill him."

"Care for a shot?" Captain Federer asked as the twosome came to his office and took a seat.

"Pardon?" Fritz asked as he and Richard stared blankly, Fred being a teetotaler.

"Kidding," he smiled with a puff of smoke. "I told you two that drinking would bite you in the butt. I tell that to all you crazy kids. You should be more like Jim. He'd never get suckered into something like that."

"We're going down to the coast to get this sorted out," Richard told him. "We'll take the Crazy Eight. We trust you won't be needing us right away."

"No, we got Airmobile and the Air Force running sorties along the DMZ on the hour while we get the Minefield back in order. There must have been three battalions pushing through here. We dug a mass grave with a bulldozer, and burned about two hundred of the ones we pulled off the barbed wire. We recovered dozens of the mats they threw over the concertina to make their way. You know how they retrieve their wounded and dead when they can, so we'll never know how many actually went down."

"Think they're coming back?" Richard asked.

"Not any time soon. You know Charlie hates invitations. Jim and I agree with your idea. If you boys hit the coast and Jim presses along the border, it'll be like squeezing zits. It may get messy but they'll be gone when all is said and done. For now."

"Burning zombies?" Richard asked before leaving.

"You know, Fritz was prattling on about zombies while he was passed out, just like you," Fred exhaled a stream of smoke. "You two watching movies while you were swilling that rotgut?"

The Legend of Green River had been passed down by generations of Vietnamese for centuries. The villagers believed that the souls of the damned entered the Green River upon burial as it traveled underground to the depths beneath the South China Sea. From there it flowed to the gates of Hell. Only during Thang Co Hon (*Ghost Month) were the gates of Hell opened so that ghosts and spirits could roam free during that time.

The souls of the departed were branded by the demons before they made their trip from the grave. The damned were marked by a green X across their faces so that they could never leave the bottomless pit. All those untouched awaited Ghost Month, and their descendants made sacrifices to the gods so that those souls could anticipate a speedy release when that time came.

Those who lived at Hamlet II by Dong Ha retired in nervous anticipation that evening. Their group consisted of twenty-four men, two squads of RFPF recruited from villages destroyed in II Corps. They were tasked to build the hamlet before their families were brought in. Only they had been compromised by the VC, and Chink Abesamis now gave the order for them to assist VC guerrillas arriving by sea to attack the base. Their hosts had been severely crippled by the failed siege and would wreak great vengeance in reprisal.

The VC guerrillas arrived at midnight, their fishing boat loaded with a twelve-man squad carrying automatic rifles and grenades. They landed at the prescribed destination and used a camouflaged fishing net to make the boat appear as moss-covered rocks. They moved silently in pairs, spreading themselves thin so as not to attract attention. They knew the building project was but fifty yards from shore and expected to see its silhouette in a short time.

As they closed in on their destination, they sensed all was not in order. They saw a couple of campfires at the town center with four figures reclined about them. The VC approached with hand signals dictating their advance. They rushed forth to rouse their new comrades as the others sought out those who remained in their barracks.

"Aieee!" a peasant cried in terror. "See these men! They have already been marked for death!"

A more experienced comrade hissed angrily as he barged past the frightened man. His beady eyes bulged as he beheld the slime-green X covering the dead man's face. Two other riflemen inspected the other prone figures and saw that they also had the mark.

"Superstitious fools," a team leader growled. "This is the work of the white dogs. They have killed their own lackeys in order to intimidate us."

"If it was the white man, why is he not firing on us?" a squat man asked. "Nay, it is the great slaughter of the other night that has caused this. As it is written, when the bowels of Hell are full, the dead shall walk the earth."

"Your head is full of shit, and I suspect your britches as well," a goateed man ridiculed him. "Remember that the white dog must report to his master after obeying each command. If they were the authors of this crime, then they have returned to their kennels. Let us split our forces. One group will return to the beach and stand guard over our boat lest the white man discovers it. The rest of us will wait here and see if any of our new comrades return from hiding."

"Agreed," a tall man waved to his team, who accompanied him as they returned to the woods surrounding the hamlet.

The goatee watched moodily as his teammates disappeared into the shadows. Three of his men joined him by the campfire as the other two searched for survivors or anyone in hiding. He knew that the white men and their Republican lackeys had narrowly escaped destruction during the siege the other night. The NVA deployed a division that provided cover by means of rocket and mortar fire as the VC patriots negotiated the Minefield. They had come within meters of the fenceline before the NVA was dislodged by the white devils' air and artillery strikes. All was not lost, however. This new campaign against their rear positions would reap great harvest.

Goatee grew impatient after long minutes passed. He was about to order a fighter to inquire before he saw six men carrying bodies on their shoulders in emerging from the shadows. He was about to belittle them for wasting their strength and energy before the men threw the corpses onto the dirt. The VC then watched in disbelief as the men dropped on their bellies behind the dead and began firing at the guerrillas.

"Ambush!" Goatee screamed. "Let us --- ohhh!"

He stared at an arrow protruding from his heart before he fell dead to the ground. The other insurgents began to raise their weapons but could not respond in time. The attackers availed themselves of the campfire, gunning the VC down as silhouettes on a target range.

"Think the others'll circle back?" Fritz Hammer mused as the attackers came forth from cover.

"I doubt it," Richard Mc Cain replied. "They know if they lose their ride, they'll be in a world of hurt. They'll have to go back to wherever they came from by foot, and that's not a great option. It's all jungle due south of here."

"I found what you wanted," Y Gal came from one of the huts with a can and a brush. He came over and handed the bucket to Richard, who grinned wolfishly as he inspected it.

"Yeah, this is gonna work," Richard nodded. "Okay, fellows, it's curtain time."

The Warriors gathered around and Fritz told them what the next phase of the game plan would be. They shrugged noncommittally and waited as Richard and Fritz painted green crosses on each others' faces, then applied the same to the Eight.

They continued on the hunt.

The VC guerrillas heard the gunfire and stopped in their tracks, unsure as to their next move.

"Listen! Our brothers may have fallen into a trap!" a slender man said anxiously.

"There couldn't have been a firefight, there weren't enough shots to have killed six men," the squad leader grunted. "They may have put some people out of their misery. Doubtlessly the white man invaded the post and killed our colleagues. Those superstitious peasants would think devils came and marked the bodies. They were partially correct --- it was white devils, for sure."

"We have to get them out of there lest we fall into a trap," a husky man insisted. "This plan's turning to shit. The Americans found out that Abesamis turned the hamlet and killed everyone. We don't know how it happened, all we know is it did. Let us send someone back and tell Dung to get his men out of there. We need to get back on the boat and return to base. This operation is screwed, I tell you."

"You're right," the leader agreed. "Hung, go back and tell Dung to pull out. Lap, you take a man and secure the boat. One of you go with Hung, Nhat will remain here with me and stand guard."

"Nyahhh!" a fighter screamed in terror. "Look! The walking dead!"

The Vietnamese stared in horror as two half-naked men shuffled as zombies toward them. They both had a green X marking their faces.

"Kill them!" the leader ordered.

"They are unarmed," Lap held out his arm. "They are obviously not white, they are our brethren. Perhaps they escaped the white devils."

"You do as I say!" the leader barked. "Go secure the boat! I'll handle this."

The leader paused to consider the situation as Lap and his partner disappeared into the brush. The rest moved hesitantly toward the zombies that continued staggering forth.

"They might as well be dead," Hung raised his rifle.

At once the zombies fell flat on their faces. Behind them a volley of arrows zipped through the air, ripping into the guerrillas. Richard and Fritz leaped over the Warriors and rushed to the fallen, slitting their throats for good measure.

"Damn, this zombie angle works pretty good," Richard chuckled as he wiped the gore from his machete on the shirt of the prostrate squad leader.

"Yeah, can't complain," Fritz nodded, studying the treeline ahead of them.

"Say, about the zombies," Richard said softly. "Remember the other night? They said we got poisoned and passed out. But I distinctly recall..."

"So do I," Fritz said ominously. "I suggest we let it slide. Unless you want Uncle Fred to put us in for a Section Eight."

"But you remember," Richard seemed as if having an epiphany.

"Do *you* remember what they said about when nobody sees it happen?"

"Yeah," Richard smiled softly. "It never happened."

"Let's go get those little shits before they slip away."

The team spread out, Richard and Fritz leading packs of four in separate directions as they entered the brush. They crept stealthily through the foliage, scrutinizing the shadows ahead for signs of enemy. At length they saw a large patch of moonlight and realized they were nearing the seashore.

Richard and Fritz exchanged signals before moving out of the bushes. They were thirty yards from the boat, where the guerrillas were pulling the camouflage net from the boat. Only the silence was disrupted by a volley of automatic fire from sand dunes on both sides. The team watched as the enemy fell to the beach in pools of blood.

"Drop your weapons!" a voice called out. "You're completely surrounded. Drop your weapons or we open fire."

The team had no problem in complying as the voices were American. The rifles, bows and arrows were at their feet as they watched the shadowy figures emerge from the surrounding reef. The team was impressed as they saw the green faces of the men in camouflage approaching.

"Wow," Richard grinned. "Damn. Now *here's* the walking dead."

"The Walking Dead are the 1/9 Marines," the leader came up to them. "That's old school. We're the new breed. Sgt. Slaughter, Navy SEALS (*Sea Air Land Commandos)."

"Yeah, well, don't forget we're the standard bearers," Fritz said as the team picked up their weapons. "Special Forces, Dong Ha."

"There's rumors the Pentagon's coming up with a new angle," Slaughter replied. "Delta Force. They're gonna roll us all up in the same ball of shit."

"And stink just as bad," Richard grunted. "I hope you don't have orders to take out that village. Takes a lot of work to put it up. No reason why we can't move a new batch of refugees in to carry on."

"Agreed," Slaughter nodded as his men came forth. They proceeded to paint green crosses on the faces of the dead. "We'll throw gasoline on these assholes and light them up. The gooks'll find them and freak out. See, the Commies don't believe in God, this don't have any bearing on them. That's why they can commit all those atrocities. They don't believe in hereafter or judgment. The villagers are a different story. They believe in angels and devils, no matter how goofy their religion is. When they see shit like this, they think it's supernatural. That makes them wanna join our side."

"Yeah, we got our own way of doing things," Fritz shrugged. "We hang their asses out to dry."

"That thing out near the Maryknoll massacre," Slaughter squinted. "Was that you?"

"Ask no questions, tell no lies."

"Oo-kayyy," Slaughter chuckled. "Just one more thing. About the report your people filed in the report on the NVA blitz on your camp. Your skipper reported a battalion getting fried. The intel we intercepted from the NVA said they lost a division. What's that about?"

"Something our skipper taught us. If no one saw it, it didn't happen."

"Divine intervention, huh?"

"Something like that."

"So, we're pretty well done for the night," Slaughter noted. "One thing about frogmen, we do enjoy our leisure time. We got a hog we're about to roast and a couple of bottles of Jack Daniels to wash it down with. Care to join us?"

"Yeah, I think we're free for the rest of the evening," Richard agreed.

And so they prepared two bonfires at considerable distance from one another. The bodies of the VC burned at one end while the commandos made merry along the opposite side of the beach. A mile away along the coastline, Coast Guard vessels fired off flares to make it seem as if Fourth of July had arrived a couple of months early.

5

LAURA

Richard arrived for coffee before dawn and saw the Montagnards setting up a miniature golf course alongside the Castle. He saw Fritz setting their mugs at the Drawbridge and casually inquired.

"The fellow who sold me the facade is going out of business and asked if I'd be interested. Do you play?"

"Not much since high school. I prefer the driving range."

"That can be arranged."

And so they loaded Fritz's golf bag and drove with Y Pes and Y Ste to a mountain bluff overlooking the South China Sea. They brought a folding table and chairs along with a lawn umbrella and the makings for mint julep. The Montagnards spent the afternoon hunting and roasting small game while the commandos worked on their driving form.

At first the commuters along the beachfront road gave sporadic reports of golf ball-sized hail by the coast. Eventually calls came in that the flurries did not consist of hail. Recon helicopters were eventually dispatched, but the golfing party had left for the day.

Richard and Fritz got a call from the Post, and arrived at the Captain's trailer where Federer's office was billowing with cigar smoke.

"This sinks it!" Fred railed at them as they took seats before his desk. "What is wrong with you two? If you're not decorating the jungle with Charlie body parts, you're playing tic-tac-toe with KIA (*Killed In Action). Now this."

"This what?" Fritz asked innocently.

"You put a golf ball through the window of a Coast Guard patrol boat. You were *this close* to having them drop fire on you."

"That was him," Richard jerked a thumb. "I can't drive that far."

"No, you," Fritz shook his head.

"Enough," Fred slapped his palm on the desk. "You're both going for four days of R&R. I know Fritz has his parents in Bismarck and Richard's got a brother in Duluth. I got you both round-trip tickets."

"I was thinking Disneyland," Richard frowned.

"I haven't been to Las Vegas," Fritz mused.

"You two adrenaline junkies are gonna get some peace and quiet, no ifs, ands or buts about it," Fred ordered. "Your plane leaves in two hours, so get packing."

By the next day, Richard found himself at Duluth International Airport. He almost felt as if he had been transported to another planet. He caught a cab and was driven downtown, yet it took a couple of hours before he made a phone call.

"Richard! How are you, little brother? Dang, we've got a great connection for a change."

"Yeah, well, I just flew into town," he swallowed hard and

fought to keep from choking at the sound of Jake Mc Cain's voice.

"What?" Jake was incredulous. "Where are you? What time are you coming over?"

"I --- I need some time," Richard rasped. "I'll be there in a bit. You know how it is."

"It's Richard," he heard Jake speaking away from the receiver to his wife Cindy. "Hey, guy, we want to see you. We love you. Don't do this."

"I'll be there, I swear," Richard assured him. "Let me get squared away, do me the favor. Tell Cindy I love her. I love you, bro. I'll get settled in and I'll call you back."

"Don't keep us waiting. Don't leave us hanging, promise?"

"I promise. See you soon."

He had checked in at the Holiday Inn, and laid on the bed in the silence trying to decompress. He finally decided to visit the lounge for a drink, and changed from his dress uniform to his blue suit and tie. After a couple of trips to the living room mirror, he felt assured he would fit in among the civilian population. Taking a deep breath, he locked the door to his room and caught the elevator to the grade level.

He took stock of the situation before finding a table along the wall in a far corner. It was the typical hotel lounge with soft lights blending across the split-level seating area. It featured a dance floor and a compact stage where a trio played bossa nova and pop tunes. A waitress took his order and brought him a shot of Jack Daniels and a Guinness. He knocked down the shot and sipped his stout, observing all who came to and fro.

"I told you I left it in the car," he heard a female voice raised from a table near the dance floor.

"Well, go get it," a male voice was exasperated.

"You want me to go by myself? Good. What a gentleman."

"Great, let's leave your sister here. Real nice. Okay, kid, we'll be right back."

"I'll be fine."

The woman agreed as her companions left the table. She seemed uncertain as she glanced around the room, watching the couple disappear down the outer hall. By the time she turned back to her drink, she was startled by the sight of the man seated across from her.

"Who are *you*?"

"Hotel security."

"Why --- is there a problem?"

"Just kidding. Thought I'd have a word before your friends return. Keep you company, as they say."

There was something about the man that intrigued her. He was of athletic build, with a thick auburn mane and smoldering chestnut eyes. His gaze exuded confidence, yet he looked upon her as if it was a spiritual experience for him.

"Richard Mc Cain."

"Laura Mueller," she extended her hand and shook his gentle grip firmly. "Are you here on business?"

"Visiting my brother and his wife. My boss decided I needed time off, so he kinda sent me over here. I just got in a couple of hours ago."

"Have you been here before?"

"It's been awhile. Say, care to dance?"

"Um...sure, okay."

She was trying to process the situation and rationalized the fact that she was routinely asked to dance whenever she attended nightclubs and seldom refused. Yet this man was different. He moved with a feline grace unusual for a man six feet in height. There was also an aura of energy emanating from him, the like of which she had never felt. It seemed to radiate from his eyes as he studied her features.

He was caught off-guard as they held each other in the dance. She was five-seven, her thick chestnut hair reaching halfway down her back. She had beautiful dark eyes, a cute nose and Cupid's bow lips, along with an hourglass waist, a generous bosom and long, lovely legs. Her dark blue dress fully complemented her delightful figure. He had met and courted many beautiful women in his life, but none like this one.

They danced to two numbers before he escorted her back to the table. Awaiting them were her companions, who were intrigued as he held her chair before sitting alongside her.

"Richard Mc Cain," he shook hands.

"I'm Joe Webster. This is my wife, Laura's sister Terri."

"I guess you happened to spot each other," Terri smiled. She was very pretty, but not like her younger sister.

"I guess you can say that," Richard smiled.

"Where do you know each other from?" Joe asked.

"We just met," Richard decided to tip his hand. "I'm in town on leave."

"Oh?" Terri was taken aback. "What kind of work do you do?"

"I'm a professional fighting man."

"Like a boxer?" Joe tried to assimilate this situation.

"I'm with Special Forces. I'm stationed in I Corps in Vietnam."

"Really?" Joe raised an eyebrow, deciding to call his bluff. He was very familiar with current events and kept abreast of the Vietnam War. "What area?"

"I'm at a fortified hamlet outside of Dong Ha near the DMZ."

"Wow, that's tough," he said softly, then waved his hand nervously. "Hey, I didn't mean it like that. I just meant there's a lot of action out that way. No offense."

"None taken. Say, uh, I'm getting shipped back in a couple

of days, and I was kinda wondering if I might ask Laura to have a drink with me. It's been a while since I've enjoyed the company of such a classy lady. I'm good company and guaranteed safe."

All they could do was look to Laura. They knew that this might well be a dead man in the next few days, weeks or months. Who could tell.

"Why, uh---" she was entirely caught off balance.

"Actually, Terri left her wallet at home," Joe revealed. "We went to check the car and it wasn't there. It'll take us an hour to go home and back. Will that work for you?"

"That would be wonderful," Richard smiled broadly.

They took full advantage of the Q&A time to get to know each other better. Both were the youngest of two siblings. Laura's parents lived in the suburbs while Richard's were deceased. Richard joined the military after graduating high school while Laura attended night courses at community college. She worked days as a librarian while determining her future path in life. Her family was of the Episcopalian faith. Both she and Richard were politically conservative, and they kept their opinions to themselves during this turbulent time in America.

Richard took her number and returned upstairs to his room. He called Beat Shit Green and left a message, which was shortly returned. Green gave him some numbers to his connections in the Duluth area. He then called Laura the next morning and set up a date at the lounge for that evening. He asked her to invite Terri and Joe as well. He then called Jake and Cindy and asked them to come out as well.

"Just so you know, you're coming back with us," Jake insisted. "You're not spending one more night in a darn motel."

He next took a cab back to the airport and headed to the

car rental office. He picked up a black Corvette Sting Ray with a military discount, and took it for a spin along Highway 535 before returning to the hotel. He parked it at the garage then headed to the gym for a workout before taking an hour-long walk around town. He had supper before returning for a nap, then watched the news until 7 PM when the meeting was set.

He found the current state of affairs highly annoying. The hippies and their left-wing supporters were the worst of the lot. The anti-war rhetoric on every major network nearly put him out of touch with society and culture. He had long accepted the fact that Democrats and the Pentagon had been painted as war mongers being manipulated by global corporations. It angered him that the war crimes of the VC were entirely ignored, as were the humanitarian achievements of MACV. Instead the Americans were depicted as murderers, and the Green Berets the worst of the lot. Yet he found it amusing that not one peacenik looked crooked at him no matter where he went in uniform.

He was concerned that Laura might think poorly if he showed up in the same suit. He made a call and had a black suit and tie with a white silk shirt brought to the room before he went downstairs for the get-together.

He walked into the lounge and saw the two couples seated with Laura at the same table as the previous night. He beamed as he came to greet them. They rose from their seats, and Cindy fell sobbing into his arms, Richard held her close, stroking her back soothingly.

"Now, c'mon, Cindy, you said you wouldn't do this," Jake held a hand toward her.

"I can't help it," she wept terribly. "I watch the news every night, I get so scared, I pray every single day. Oh, Richard, thank God you're back here with us."

"Omigosh," Terri broke into tears, Joe putting a consoling arm around her.

Cindy sank into her chair, and the brothers grabbed each other by the lapels. They stared into each others' eyes before grabbing each other in a fiercely loving bear hug.

"Okay, girls, I think we should go powder our noses," Laura managed, finding herself nearly overcome. Terri patted Cindy's shoulders, and she rose to accompany the sisters to the ladies' room.

"This guy," Jake hugged his brother's shoulders as the men resumed their seats. "We hadn't heard from him all summer outside of a couple of postcards and birthday cards."

"C'mon, now, I send cards every holiday," Richard corrected him.

"Gee, thanks," Jake was sarcastic. "So they have that Tet Offensive right around the holidays. Walter Cronkite's going nuts, the networks are showing all these battle scenes, they're running all these casualty numbers, everybody's saying the war's lost, And not a word from my little brother. Finally, on Christmas Eve, we get a call. The operator puts us through, and this guy comes on asking if we're going to the Minnesota North Stars game."

"Oh, man," Richard rolled his eyes. "Now you know I asked you how you and Cindy were first."

"There," Jake was exasperated. "See?"

"I can see how Cindy might've been concerned," Joe's expression gave his understatement away.

They ordered shots and clinked glasses in a toast before the women returned. Laura walked around the table where Richard stood to meet her.

"Well, hi there," she smiled. They hugged each other, and everyone immediately was struck by what a perfect couple they made.

"Now I can die happy," he came over and kissed Cindy on the head before he sat down. "This is heaven."

"Yeah," Jake grimaced at him. "You die and I'll dig you up and kick your butt."

With that Cindy gave him a hard slap across the arm. The ensuing laughter broke the tension, and soon everybody was in the process of getting acquainted. Jake was a schoolteacher and Joe worked for a publishing company. They began discussing how Joe might get Jake's school board some new books at a discount. Terri was delighted to learn that she and Cindy went to the same health club. They began making plans to meet for their evening workouts.

Richard and Laura engaged in quiet conversation until he finally rose to his feet.

"Say, I'm gonna take Laura for a ride in my Sting Ray," he announced. "I'll have her back to Joe's by midnight. And I'll be heading straight back to Jake's afterward."

"You got that right, soldier boy," Jake teased him. Richard and Laura exchanged hugs with everyone before departing.

Laura had gone on infrequent casual dates over the past couple of years. She had been courted by classmates, and most drove Volkswagens or station wagons. The only time she rode in luxury cars was when she went out with her parents. She had never taken a ride in a Sting Ray and was quite impressed. He opened her door for her before hopping in, gunning the engine and sailing on down the road.

"So where are we going?" she wondered, noticing they were heading away from downtown.

"My Army buddy gave me an address along Fourth Street. Are we heading the right way?"

"Well...yeah," she said uncertainly.

They cruised by a social club in front of which a small group of young black men were congregating. Richard backed up and parked perfectly between two vehicles a couple of doors down. Laura was uncertain as this was known as an area frequented by drug dealers.

"Are you sure you have the right address?" she asked as he came around and opened her door.

"Sure am," he replied. "My friend Beat...uh...Sgt. Green gave me the directions. Highly recommended."

They walked up to the entrance and got the once over as they were confronted by the doorman.

"You looking for somebody?" the hulking black man asked.

"No, I got recommended."

"By who?"

"Beat Shit Green, 25th Infantry."

"You mean Sgt. Walter Green?"

"Uh,,,yeah."

"And who might you be?"

"Sgt. Richard Mc Cain, 5th Special Forces Group."

"Well," the man's face and voice softened. "Why didn't you say so? Leroy, show these people inside and get them a table."

The pastel-colored walls with soft lighting seemed as a rundown version of the Holiday Inn lounge. They were shown to a table near a small dais where a blues band was playing lively Fifties classics. The manager came over as the waiter brought drinks, informing them the round was on the house.

"Sorry for the confusion," he smiled broadly. "Sgt. Green called last night and said you were coming. He failed to mention you were white."

"Typical Beat Shit," Richard shook his head as he touched glasses with Laura.

"Why on earth do you call him that?" she wondered.

"Well, uh...long story short...erm...I'd best explain later."

"So what is it you do where you're stationed?"

"We help the local people defend their village. We provide

medical services and make sure they're getting the food and supplies they need."

"Kinda like the Red Cross, huh?"

"Something like that."

"You've got to have a caring heart to provide for people like that. You don't get involved in a lot of fighting doing what you do...do you?"

"Not more than most other units. You know how the media blows everything out of proportion. It's like they say, believe half of what you see and half of what you hear."

"Well, I'm very glad to hear that," she gave him a smile that made his heart skip a beat. "I don't even want to think about you being involved in any of those battles they show on TV."

"Not me," he reassured her. "We've got a saying. The smart fellows stay in the rear with the gear. That's me all over. Especially now that I've got such a lovely new friend on the Stateside. I wouldn't want to come back here with a black eye and bumps on my head."

"Well, I wouldn't want that either," her laughter touched his heart as a wind chime.

"Say," Richard called a waiter. "Where's the action?"

"Right down back, through the black curtain."

Richard took her hand and led her to the rear of the club.

"What action?" she asked as they slipped through the curtain.

It was as if entering another world, or a different set at a Hollywood studio. The patrons were packed tightly alongside one another at the crowded bar and the gambling tables. Once again Laura felt unsure in realizing that she and Richard were the only white people in the room. She dismissed her apprehensions in knowing that she had lived a sheltered existence and seldom mingled with those of different classes and ethnicities outside the suburbs.

"Hey, we got another roller at the table," the croupier announced. "Hand this man the bones."

Richard stepped up and produced one of the two rolls of bills he brought with him. He had left the rest of the score he got from Buffalo Bill back in Saigon for safekeeping. Laura took a glimpse at the wad and nearly broke a cold sweat.

"You shouldn't be showing that much money in a place like --- in public," she said quietly.

"It's gotten a bit thin since I came to town," he peeled a $100 bill off the top and dropped it on the table. "Let's see what we can do about that."

She was filled with consternation as the dice was shoveled over with a rattan stick. She had never seen anyone risk that kind of money in a game before. She knew the Army did not pay soldiers a good salary, and his brother was a schoolteacher. She hoped he had not brought his savings along on this trip.

"What happened?" she asked after he rolled the dice across the felt table.

"We made an eight," he explained. "The highest possibility of combinations is seven and eleven. If you hit them on the first roll you win. After that, if you roll them you lose. If you roll any other combination, you have to roll them again to win."

"And if you roll seven or eleven again, the easiest to hit, you lose."

"Right."

"Can you get a refund?"

She watched breathlessly as he rolled the dice three times without hitting a seven or eleven. On the fourth roll he hit an eight and was shoveled ten $20 bills.

"Omigosh," she sighed in relief. "Don't play any more."

"Well, now, I wouldn't be a gentleman if I didn't let you have a roll."

"Oh, no, I couldn't," she said before he pressed the dice into her hand.

"Lady on the line, place your bets," the croupier announced. Laura realized she had no choice but to throw the dice. Again she was startled as Richard threw the $200 on the table.

"Eleven," the croupier announced. "The lady hits eleven."

"Wow," she said after she collected the winnings. "Nice."

"Here, put it in this envelope and hold it for me," he entreated her. "I'll explain later."

She was bemused as she managed to wedge the stack of bills into the envelope he gave her. She slipped it in her purse, hoping she would not get knocked on the head for it. They returned to the main lounge area and had a couple of drinks before it was time for him to bring her to her sister's home. He would make sure that he brought her back right on time on their first date.

They pulled up in front of the Websters' ranch house along the outskirts of Duluth. Richard realized they were not far from where Jake and Cindy lived. He hoped they had made a connection before leaving the Holiday Inn.

"I had a wonderful time," she said as he helped her from the sports car.

"I'll give you a call tomorrow," he assured her.

He walked her up to the front door. As expected, the porch lights came on as Joe and Terri came out to greet them.

"Hope you two had a great time," Joe smiled.

"It was quite interesting," Laura assured them. "And I'm pretty sure I'm never been in more capable hands."

"Hmm," Terri cocked an eyebrow, evoking a playful slap on the arm from Laura.

"Thanks for taking care of Little Sister," Joe grinned.

"I gave you the envelope back, didn't I," Laura said quietly as Richard hugged her and kissed her cheek.

"Sure did," he said. "I'll call you tomorrow around noon."

He then hugged and kissed Terri before shaking hands with Joe and giving him a quick hug as well.

"Drive safe, big guy," Joe said as Richard returned to the Corvette and streaked off.

"Well, look who's got stars in their eyes," Terri teased. She had not seen her little sister as ebullient in quite some time.

"Yeah, he's something else," Laura managed.

"Hey, what's this?" Joe reached in his evening robe pocket and inspected the contents. "Huh. I guess this belongs to you. Got your name on it."

He handed Laura the envelope containing the $400.

All she could do was shake her head.

He certainly was full of surprises.

6

THE STING

Richard returned to Dong Ha a couple of days after his date with Laura. He spent the following day with Jake and Cindy, and the next day in the skies flying halfway back around the planet. In essence, the four-day furlough was actually half travel, half R&R.

He knew what overseas relationships were like as evidenced by his brothers in arms. There was the new romance, the recruits who carried the pics of their sweethearts as holy relics in their wallets and waited for incoming mail as dogs wishing for a bone. The husbands and dads became pious, praying to God to watch over their families and that they would return home in one piece. Those whose families could not endure were the most wretched, degenerate alcoholics whose death wish made them the most dangerous of all.

He met Fritz for coffee at dawn and was invited inside the Castle. They recognized a reticence about one another and sensed they had some unique experiences during their time off. They continued to exchange anecdotes about their airline flights until Fritz finally came clean.

"I never told you my Dad was Waffen SS."

"No, you mentioned that your parents came over after the War and that he served in the German Army," Richard recalled. "I was heavily into military history in high school, you know. I know the Waffen SS were the hardcore players."

"Yes, he was with the Leibstandarte. Backpedaled all the way from Stalingrad to Berlin. He surrendered to the Americans and cut a deal with the OSS (*Office of Strategic Services) to help extract rocket scientists from Russian territory. That got him a green card. As we know, the OSS evolved into the CIA. They found out I was in Special Forces and reached out to him. He got me in touch, so I'm loosely connected."

"So what, you're a spook?"

"No, just a connected guy. They reached out to me and asked if I could help them on a job. They asked if I knew anyone I could trust."

'Now let me guess," Richard gazed up at the ceiling.

"Only thing about this, it's strictly God and country," Fritz said flatly. "You'll earn credits with the Company, Other than that, this work never happened. If the music stops and we don't have seats, we get left holding the bag. Period."

"No RK's (*registered kills), no medals, nothing for our dossier," Richard smiled. "Par for the course, I reckon. Okay, God and country. Who do we have to kill?"

"It's kind of a sting operation against the Russians."

"That's a no-can-do," Richard frowned. "I don't mess with Russians."

"What?" Fritz squinted.

"Kidding," Richard scoffed. "Man, you should see your face."

"Well, I've got a thing about Russians. I've got family in East Germany that my Dad can't get out, even with his connections."

"Like they say, an enemy of yours is an enemy of mine. So keep talking."

"We know the Russians are conducting a proxy war here just like the Chinese. *Deus ex machina*, as they say. Anyway, the KGB is trying to move two million dollars worth of AK-47's, but the VC's having trouble coming up with the money. They did a bait and switch with an offer to sell them two million worth of heroin from the Golden Triangle. The logic was that they could make the big investment, then earn their money back to buy the rifles. Only there's one fellow who thinks he can have his cake and eat it too. As Bob Dylan might say."

Fritz unlocked a file cabinet in a far corner and brought a folder over to the coffee table.He opened it to show a photo which he laid before Richard.

"This is Can Cun."

"Huh. I think they named a place in Mexico after him."

"Whatever. He's a Chinese national suspected of being involved with everything from gun running to drug trafficking, gambling, prostitution, you name it. He's got strong connections to the Ministry of State Security in China as well as Vietnamese government officials. His official title is Vice-President with Shanghai Imports and Exports. He's been untouchable so far. Only the Company thinks the Russians are making him an offer he can't refuse."

"How so?"

"Every man's got a weakness, so they say. This fellow's a gambling man. They say when he shows up at a casino, it's like a wet dream for the owners. He bets big, tips big and wins big. Matter of fact, the Company thinks he wins too big."

"Cheats?"

"That's the angle. The big dogs think he works the game months in advance. He gets to a pit boss at a target joint and moves in when he's sure the dealer is beyond reproach. After he scores, he makes sure his guy stays in until the smoke clears. Pit bosses are in demand, always on the move. New casinos are always looking for card sharks and will pay top dollar. The casino owners are always on the lookout, but you can't pull your top dealer when a guy like Can Cun comes by. They have their eagles watching the table, but so far he's never been caught."

"So the Company thinks they're gonna take him down?"

"That's the objective. They've got a guy from England who plays all the big casinos in Europe, well known in Monte Carlo. They're planning to bring him in when Can Cun shows, and when word gets out it'll be the biggest game in town. They're already baiting the trap by making it RSVP exclusive. They'll set it up so Can Cun can put a million on the table and try to double it to finance the Russian deal."

"And if we can sting him, both the VC and the Russians are screwed."

"Precisely."

The opening phase of the operation required them to meet with contacts in Saigon for the set-up. They came to Captain Federer's office to discuss the situation and were pleased to learn that the CIA had already made arrangements with MACV. A helicopter arrived within a couple of hours, and they were transported to III Corps shortly thereafter.

They arrived at the military airport and were driven by taxi to the Saigon Hotel located in the heart of the downtown area. They were booked in adjoining luxury suites and given $1,000 credit cards to enhance their profiles. They were advised in advance that they would be held accountable for the expenditures on Uncle Sam's account. When they arrived at their suite, they were pleased to find clothing and accessories having been provided for them.

The game was scheduled for the following evening. Only the operatives were appointed to meet tonight to review the game plan. Richard and Fritz were instructed to arrive at the lobby bar by 7 PM where the Englishman would join them. They dressed casually and ordered drinks at the bar where only a handful of customers were seen.

At length a tall, tiger-muscled man entered the lounge and strolled over to where they stood. He had dark hair, piercing eyes and a sturdy jaw. He seemed as if a fitting counterpart to the Americans in matching height and build.

"I believe we have an appointment," he smiled softly. "My name is Bomb. James Bomb."

The partners looked at each other for a long moment before breaking into raucous laughter.

"I'm sorry," he squinted, briefly glancing over his shoulder, "Did I...?"

"No, no, no," Richard held up a hand. "We were expecting you. I'm Mr. Goldfinger, and this is Oddjob."

"Enough with the ribs," Fritz retorted. "He's Mickey Oddjob. I'm Goldfinger."

"Should I come back in and start over?" the Englishman cocked an eyebrow.

"Don't mind us, we've had a few," Richard alibied. "C'mon, let's take that table in the back. There's three more people we'll be waiting on."

James ordered a drink from their waiter at the table as Richard and Fritz asked for refills of their double shots of Jack Daniels. At length they were joined by two more guests. Kung Pao was a Chinaman who was well known along the hotel circuit as an experienced hospitality worker. Moo Goo Gai was another Chinese national with a strong reputation along the underworld as a card shark. They engaged in light conversation until the sixth member of the team arrived.

They heard the sharp clicking of high heels on the highly-buffed lounge floor before catching sight of an attractive

Vietnamese woman in a tight emerald dress and black nylons toting a gaudy oversized purse that resembled a small shopping bag. It was silver-beaded and featured four circular ornaments on both side that were almost as opaque mirrors.

"Loki," Richard and Fritz were taken aback. "What are you doing here?"

"Captain Fred hooked me up for a temporary assignment," she explained, taking a seat at the table. "He got me a ride and had the clothes and room paid for. You like?"

"That bag looks like he sent you down here to go shoplifting," Richard said, causing her to frown and slap his arm.

"Okay, everybody has an inkling of why we're here, though we may not know who sent whom for what," Fritz opened the discussion. "Let's keep it that way. What we do know is that there's a high-stakes poker game tomorrow. Six players coming in at a fifty grand ante, no refunds. Everyone who taps out forfeits the ante. That means the big winner walks away with three hundred grand, not counting table stakes."

"Good to know your government has that much confidence in your skills," Moo was sardonic.

"More like they're confident in the potential of this team," Fritz replied. "The mark we're working is playing with money he doesn't have. He's gambling on winning to make a deal he can't afford. If he walks away a winner, the people of South Vietnam will be very, very big losers."

"So why not just make sure he never reaches the table?" Moo wondered.

"The money he doesn't have belongs to some very dangerous people. We want to get our hands on this money. Now, everybody knows the game's being played at the Golden Phoenix tomorrow night. We also know what kind of place it is. They are protected from the government level to the local police and the underworld. If anyone gets caught trying to work this game, rest assured you will end up in Chi Hoa Prison. Us Yanks will get to go to Long Binh Jail en route to Leavenworth. If I end up there because of any of you, pray to your triple-headed gods that I never find you when you get out."

"Obviously I've been brought in to outplay the mark," James mused. "And you two Yanks are expected to narrow the field against whoever else is at the table. Of course, Moo will be a last resort. So just as obviously, the post-game becomes the end game. No matter who wins, the loser will most likely do whatever it takes to get their money back."

"As far as this team's concerned, your assignment is completed once the chips are cashed in. We'll provide an escort for James to make sure the winnings end up in the right place."

"Just to make sure no one has any ambitions as to what they might be able to do with two million dollars," James smiled.

"Precisely."

"Well, I hope there's enough left over to pay for dinner and a show," Loki insisted. "I hope I didn't fly all the way to Saigon just to wait tables for a couple of hours."

The Golden Phoenix was the newest addition to the bustling downtown area of Saigon. Instead of the private cabs and rickshaws that flowed through the streets in front of the other bars and casinos, spaces were reserved for limousines and official vehicles that accommodated patrons. Burly Samoans stood watch at all doorways and debonair Chinamen saw to every need. Vietnamese comprised the hospitality staff and were circulating as frenetically as the cash flow.

"You look like a used car salesman," Fritz teased Richard as they met in the hallway of their hotel after changing to their formal wear. They both wore black suits with open shirts, Fritz in goldenrod and Richard in royal blue.

"You look like a dumbwaiter. Only I don't think the lift goes back to the top."

They took the elevator to the lobby and entered the car that awaited them outside. The car took a short trip to the Phoenix where Fritz showed their passes. The valets opened their doors for them and cleared the way so that they accessed the MVP carpet into the casino.

There was a designated area on a split level that was already clogged by spectators wanting to witness this game awarding such a spectacular prize. The Samoans cleared the path so that the Americans could access the playing area. The Indian and the African awaited, and the teammates took seats at the horseshoe table facing the early arrivals.

At length the other men made their entrance. James was dressed in a white evening jacket and black tuxedo pants with a red rose on his lapel. He took a seat to the dealer's left. As soon as he did so, Can Cun made his appearance.

Richard thought it amusing that Americans often said that they could not distinguish Orientals as they all looked the same. Yet it was a challenge if he was forced to describe Can Cun. His slanted eyes were no different than others, perhaps darker than most. He had a small pug nose, yet not as compact as that of Chink Abesamis. There was a smiling mouth, not as thin-lipped as Abesamis but somewhat nondescript. He wore a pompadour, but not so distinct as any other. If he had to give a description to police, they would greatly scorn his ability as a Special Forces operative.

"Ladies and gentlemen," the emcee stepped up to a microphone. "Welcome to the poker tournament event of the year. The participants have contributed to a grand prize exceeding any in the history of this casino. This is the ultimate test of the skill and the will of those who will rise to the challenge and claim the fortune. Let us commence and see who will be the King of Seven Card Stud!"

Seven Card Stud was the most fortuitous of poker games. It allowed for three face cards to leverage against the four hole cards. Richard was well known as a fearsome poker player. Yet he was unaware of Fritz's reputation until he asked around. It was coincidental that the two of them were brought to this, yet as a Southern Baptist he did not believe in coincidence.

The game commenced and it seemed as a game as any other. Yet Richard was able to discern patterns as they appeared. Can Cun had an arrogant look whenever he was dealt a strong hand, but that was not necessarily a tell. James' eyebrows shifted but they did not indicate a pattern. The Indian Singh's eyebrows arched at every hand he was dealt. The African seemed to react to every hand as if someone passed him the note from a fortune cookie.

The first train wreck appeared as Can Cun showed a pair of kings. The black man, Ebon Kinte, held a pair of queens. Curry Singh had tens. Fritz had a pair of threes. Richard stayed in with deuces and got burned for a grand. Yet he could see the pattern. Fritz was playing against the Indian. Richard needed to adjust his game to play against the African. This would allow James to go head on against Cun.

There was a scheduled break at eight PM that allowed the participants to use the restroom, grab a snack or otherwise clear their heads. Richard and Fritz rendezvoused in the men's room to agree on their strategy and compare notes.

"Sounds good," Fritz agreed with Richard's idea. "Only we might take turns calling each others' mark if one of us has to fold. It'll keep them honest. Plus we should keep pressure on Cun when possible to give James the boost."

When they returned to the table, it appeared as if everyone

had ordered a fresh supply of chips. Stacks of $100 chips sat in front of each player's seat at the table. Richard and Fritz went with the flow, and they had $10,000 of chips in front of them as the game resumed. They were both maxed out and would have to cash in their chips if their potential losses exceeded their chances of winning. The Company was paying for their chips and it was expected they would make good.

Time was becoming a factor in the competition. There was another scheduled break at ten. By that time, it was likely that at least one player would be facing elimination. It was entirely possible that these high rollers could purchase greater amounts of chips if they were depleted. Yet they all knew a streak of poor luck could result in their throwing in good money after bad, a major taboo in the gambling world. It was more likely they would cut their losses and walk away, looking for a better day and time to return to their winning ways.

By ten PM it was clear that Cun and James were moving ahead as the big winners. It was evident by the stacks of chips piled before them. Singh was doing well but his fortunes rose and fell as he continually staved off the challenges of Fritz. Kinte was a different story. Fritz had to fold a couple of times during heavy betting, forcing Richard to make the calls. Richard won some but lost big on a hand that would cause him to retire before the next break.

"You're leaving me in a rough spot, Mickey," Fritz said as he downed a shot of Jack Daniels at the lounge bar during the break. "The Indian's playing close to the vest. I haven't got a read on him yet. The black will be a distraction. If he starts feeling strong with you gone, they may be able to leverage me."

"C'mon, Square, where's the Aryan will to power?" Richard ribbed him. "Look, I've got three grand of chips to cash in. I'll have the money transferred to your tab. The black guy's playing defense, he's not gonna play tough until Cun or James start to crack. You got the Indian on his heels. I'm seeing his eyes when you double the bet on face cards. He doesn't see you as a bluffer. You might be able to sandbag him on some big pots if Cun and James fold. Just watch the African. He may be looking for a chance to pick your bones if he calls a bluff."

"We'll see what happens," Fritz rose to return to the table. "If we lose it all, we'll be into the Company for one hundred twenty grand. We were hoping they might owe us a favor when all's said and done. Might be the other way around."

Richard was finishing his Guinness when a slender man in a black suit, tie and white shirt signaled the barmaid to set them up for another dink.

"Mr. Uno," he introduced himself without shaking hands. He wore tinted aviator shades and barely looked at Richard. "I'm with the Company."

"Came to check on the score?"

"I'll be watching for Kung Pao to make his play. I'll be positioned on the opposite side of the railing across from you. I'll be leaving right behind Pao. You count three and follow me out. We'll take it from there."

Uno downed his shot of Maker's Mark and walked off. Richard slammed his Jack Daniels and took his Guinness back to the playing area.

The game resumed with a jolt as everyone at the table was dealt formidable hands on the fifth round. Cun held a pair of queens and Fritz had a pair of jacks. Singh had a two spades while Kinte had a seven and an eight. Everyone shoveled a grand into the pot as the dealer began tossing the cards.

"Shit!' Fritz suddenly yelled as Kung Pao appeared on his left. The waiter appeared to stumble, spilling a large dollop of whiskey onto the table near Fritz's arm. Pao immediately set his tray onto the table but was unable to avoid a hollow-handed slap to his right ear. The Chinaman fell to one knee, breaking his fall on Can Cun's lap as he begged forgiveness.

"Stupid bastard," Fritz rose to his feet as two bouncers appeared. Pao cringed as Cun managed to ease the Chinaman into the arms of a bouncer. The second man took Pao's serving tray and daubed the spilled liquid with a towel as he apologized.

"Okay, I'm good," Fritz growled. "Leave that towel, put it over the mess so I don't get my arm wet."

"We can relocate you," the bouncer offered.

"Nah, I don't wanna change my luck. Just keep that guy on a leash."

The players agreed to a misdeal and reluctantly returned the promising hands to the table. Richard watched as Pao headed for the hallway, ostensibly to recover from the mishap. He waited until Mr. Uno followed Pao out before leaving his spot on the rail surrounding the gambling area. He walked out to the adjoining lounge bar and saw Uno and Pao awaiting him at the bar.

"All right, we're on the clock," Uno informed him. "Pao lifted Can Cun's wallet. I've got a man with a suitcase device that will transmit all his card info to the Office. It'll take a few minutes but I'm sure he's too engrossed in the game to notice. Once we put it back, we go to our next play. Just be ready to run interference if anything goes wrong. People have seen you with Fritz, it'll explain you going to his side if necessary."

The game continued, and the tension mounted as Fritz and Cun squared off once again. Cun was showing two kings and a jack, causing Singh and Kinte to fold. Fritz raised two grand and was rewarded with a diamond flush.

The tension was almost instantly relieved when Loki appeared in relief of Kung Pao. She was dressed in a low-cut blouse and short skirt that greatly enhanced her delightful physique. She was very chatty and assured Cun that no further mishaps would occur on her watch. She also brought a fruit drink to the dealer, who insisted he placed no order but accepted it anyway.

Fritz appeared as if he was on a roll but was immediately met head-on by Cun, who was not going to loosen control any further than what was happening with James. Fritz drew a pair of jacks but was looking at James with a pair of sevens, Cun with a ten-jack-queen possible straight, Kinte with three hearts and Singh with two tens and an ace. Fritz pushed a stack to the center of the table but was raised by Cun with two grand. Kinte and Singh seemed reluctant, but got sandbagged by James who raised to six grand. At the final draw, Fritz's three jacks were flattened by Cun's straight. Only the crowd gasped then applauded James' full house. Kinte waved off before leaving the game.

The dealer began to resume, only turned sideways as he had to clear his throat. He began coughing more violently and suddenly dropped to one knee from his seat. Two bouncers rushed to his side, causing a considerable delay. Eventually calm was restored as a new croupier arrived at the table. It was Moo Goo Gai.

The clock was ticking eleven-thirty as they moved toward the championship rounds. The ante would be set at fifty grand, which would fairly well guarantee that those remaining afloat would either sink or swim. Cun and James remained smug as the five stacks made no difference in the pile sitting before them. Fritz kept his poker face as Singh seemed hesitant but anted anyway.

Cun had three tens, and Singh was showing a nine-ten-jack. Fritz had a pair of kings to a seven, and James showed a ten-queen-ace of spades. The crowd was buzzing but grew silent when Fritz went all in. Singh was clearly uncertain but had no choice being so close to a straight. Most likely he had one in the hole, open on both ends.

"All in," Cun pushed his chips toward the center table. It was easily nine hundred grand.

"Well," James cocked an eyebrow, "one never knows unless they take a peek."

The croupier dealt and the players peeled the corners of their card to have a look. After a long moment, James turned his cards.

It was a royal flush.

Fritz and Singh tossed their hands as Can Cun turned a beet red. He knew the odds of such a draw were astronomical. He stared at Moo Goo Gai, who seemed astonied by the luck of the draw. Cun stalked off as six of his entourage emerged from the crowd and escorted him from the premises.

Richard joined James and waited patiently as the big winner cashed in his chips. The payoff came in two million dollars' worth of gold bullion set in a complimentary satchel. Richard smiled admiringly as James produced a set of handcuffs and chained himself to the case.

"This'll ensure us that no one gets any stupid ideas," James explained.

"Sounds like a winner."

Richard and James left the casino and met with two men in suits at the entrance. A valet pulled up in an Aston Martin, and the men got in front as Richard and James slipped into the rear seats. At once they were streaking down the road toward the airport.

"I'm sure your government will be quite pleased as how things went," James said as they approached the outskirts of town.

"Things will get even better," Richard grinned. "You keep looking back. Expecting anyone?"

"In my line of work, you develop a habit of looking over your shoulder," James said pointedly. "It serves to assure one that their arse will still be there in the morning."

At length a car could be seen in the distance careening in their direction at 90 MPH. As they approached an intersection, the vehicle's headlights lurched toward their path. The driver slammed on the brakes and jerked the wheel, putting the luxury car into a tailspin. Only the car hit a slick spot and careened off the road onto a steep slope.

"Dumb sonofabitch," Richard cursed the driver, a stream of blood pouring from left side of his head where he smashed the window.

"We could've been killed," the driver hissed.

"Could've?" Richard asked as he pulled a Walther PPK and shot both men in the front seats through the head. Their brains sprayed across the windshield as Richard hammered James across the temple. He was already stunned after banging his head in the crash.

Richard heard a second crash and clambered out of the car. He walked up the slope and saw where Fritz had driven his crash car into that of Can Cun, which had come to a halt in their plot to confiscate the bullion. Cun got out of his vehicle and had his skull blown apart by Fritz as he approached. Behind him, CIA agents raced up and sprayed the hijackers' car with automatic fire.

"That car you've been looking for isn't coming," Richard opened the rear passenger door where James wiped his suit sleeve on a head wound. "The CIA made you a week ago. Is it Bomb or Bomberg? East German, we presume. The Russians figured you'd work with us and play the sting. Then your guys would ambush us and get the money back. Only Can Cun had the same idea. We found that out when our guy picked his pocket."

"You're bloody mad," James garbled.

"Yeah, that's what I hear. Playtime's over. The police and ambulance are on the way. You can blame all this on Can Cun. Now, hand over the key to the cuffs and we'll be on our way."

"Look, you've got your facts seriously jumbled," James spat blood. "They're supposed to remove the cuffs at the airport when they take possession."

"Final answer?" Richard asked softly. He then grabbed James by the lapels and pulled him forth so he could grab the valise chained to the left wrist. He yanked the valise until he pulled James across the rear floorboard. He then slammed the rear driver door on James' arm with full force. James' screams intensified as Richard produced a meat cleaver and severed the hand from the cuff.

He met Fritz at the crash car and they squeezed in the back seat along with two other men. The man on the rear passenger side took the case from Richard and put it in the trunk before getting back in alongside Richard.

"This thing's beat to hell," the driver announced, steam hissing from beneath the ruptured hood.

"I saw a motel a few miles back," Mr. Uno sat in the passenger seat. "Turn around and go back. "I'll have the Office send a new car out and tow this one."

Uno introduced his cohorts as Mr. Deux, Mr. Trois and Mr. Quatro as the car wheezed back down the road.

"Any way you can have our team brought over, as long as it's safe?" Richard wondered.

"I don't see why not," Uno replied. "I'll send some backup and we'll cover your tab. All for a job well done. Just be sure not to miss your flight tomorrow. That's on the military, we don't want to know where you came from or where you're headed. Terms of the contract."

An hour later, the motel lounge closed for the evening though three new arrivals were being escorted in by staff members. A tidy sum was paid so the party of six could avail themselves of the facilities undisturbed and undetected.

Richard and Fritz were glad to see Loki, Kung Pao and Moo Goo Gai directed to the entrance. The three arrivals came to the rear table where they were hugged by the Americans before taking seats.

"Sorry about that shot to the head," Fritz gripped Kung Pao affectionately around the back of the neck. "It's what the pro wrestlers do back home. Makes lots of noise, does little damage."

"I hate to see what you do when wanting to do damage," Pao managed a smile.

"You did some job in lifting that wallet," Richard said admiringly. "I had no idea you were making that play. Gotta hand it to Fritz for setting it up. I thought that was a little over the top for him. We've been in tighter spots where he never raised an eyebrow."

"Shit!" Fritz yelled, preparing to launch a backhand. At once Pao was seated on the floor alongside him as the team broke out in laughter.

"Please don't kill me," Pao begged, rising to his knees and wrapping his arms around Fritz's waist.

"Hands off the merchandise, slope," Fritz pushed him off.

"Gotcha," Pao retreated, slapping Fritz's wallet onto the table.

"Now that's what I call a power lifter," Fritz chuckled, putting his wallet back in his pocket.

The group became nonchalant as a waiter brought a tray of drinks, followed by a Queen Mary featuring a smorgasbord of seafood and Oriental appetizers.

"So the Academy Awards ceremony continues," Fritz said in a theatrical voice. "Our nominee for Best Actress?"

"Our little Miss Low Key has my vote," Richard waved a hand.

Loki got up and did an elaborate curtsy before helping herself to a Cuba Libre and a dish of sushi and kimchee.

"So what did you slip that gook to get him to take his pratfall?" Fritz inquired.

"From what I understand, there was Drano mixed with something called Rohypnol," she raised her eyebrows apprehensively. "The Drano made him sick, then the drug knocked him down. They told me exactly what it would do so I wouldn't be alarmed or get distracted."

"You did a great job," Richard praised her. "I had no idea what was going on. Everybody at the table thought he had a medical emergency."

"You don't know the half of it," Fritz told him. "While Moo Goo was stepping up to the plate, she went over to Can Cun while nobody was looking. Tell 'em, Loki."

"Mr. Can Cun, did you drop this?" she wiggled an imaginary object in the air.

"We got his wallet back as soon as Mr. Uno got it scanned out," Fritz explained. "We figured Cun was suspicious, but he was so wrapped up in the game that he wasn't gonna act out. He might've suspected Kung Pao but would've never thought Loki was in on it. Still, when a high roller like Cun gets his wallet lifted, it creates distraction. That's where our man Moo Goo really rattles his cage."

"I thought dealing Bomb a royal flush was far out," Richard shook his head. "Right away I knew it would push Cun over the edge. When he rolled out of the casino with his boys, I knew they had something in mind."

"It was a real piece of work," Fritz nodded. "Bomberg had no idea the Company was onto him. He had a team of East German gunmen waiting in a car outside to follow his ride out to that intersection where everything happened. Mr. Uno had a unit already waiting for them. They gave us the intel along with what they picked up from Cun, who they wiretapped since the game was scheduled. The whole car wreck was a masterpiece."

"This whole story doesn't make any sense," Loki complained as she munched on her sushi. "How about we start from beginning and you tell me what happened."

"We agree," Kung Pao and Moo Goo chimed in. "Whole thing clear as mud."

"It's like they said when they hired you for the job," Richard reached out and playfully tweaked Loki's nose. "They only told you what you needed to know. All this crazy stuff, you don't need to know."

The gathering lasted until 4 AM, at which time they were all provided rooms courtesy of the Company. Richard and Fritz were given a wake-up call for them to prepare for their ride to Tan Son Nhut Air Base for a flight back to Dong Ha. As promised, Loki would be escorted at Saigon for a shopping trip before she was flown back to the International Airport at Tan Son Nhut for her return flight. Kung Pao and Moo Goo would be able to call for a ride to the airport. They would be relocated to Nha Trang for temporary work until things settled down in Saigon over the Can Cun affair.

It was something they had grown used to since their early days as recruits. They fully appreciated why the flights were referred to as the Red Eye. Only they were taken aback as they were deposited at a landing strip near a warehouse where a Hercules C-130 transport aircraft was being loaded.

"What the hell are we doing here?" Richard asked the driver.

"Orders," the man replied. "You report to the guy in charge."

Fritz strutted over to an Air Force sergeant overseeing the process as airmen were using hand trucks to bring wooden boxes onto the plane.

"We're supposed to be going to Dong Ha."

"Yep, that's our destination."

"We just completed a mission, we expected a commercial flight."

"Well, I don't see one hereabouts," the sergeant tried not to laugh. "I got word you guys can ride Space-A (*space available). We leave in twenty minutes."

"And where are our seats?"

"In the rear with the gear," the sergeant jerked a thumb at the cargo space as he walked off.

7

HALLS OF JUSTICE

The Air Force B-52's brought their own monsoons into Communist sanctuaries. They carried one hundred eight bombs, payloads providing sixty thousand pounds of explosive power, They annihilated targets not only in Vietnam but Cambodia and Laos as well. Although bombing operations were officially restricted to the Vietnamese theater of war, military commanders were loathe to recall sorties that spotted enemy troops and convoys fleeing across borders in hopes of safe refuge.

Prince Sihanouk, ruler of Cambodia, was a weak man appointed by nepotism who feared the power of the NVA and the VC running rampant throughout his border country. He was greatly troubled by the ascension of the Red Khmers who posed a political and military threat to his regime. This insurrectionist group developed through their ties with the NVA/VC network and were strengthened by the black market trade along the Ho Chi Minh Trail. They eventually built an extension that ran along the border which they mockingly christened the Sihanouk Trail.

It increased the striking ability of the enemy, allowing them to launch attacks from Cambodia with the objective being to flee across the border for safety. The NVA knew that repeated violations of the border sovereignty of Cambodia would result in protests by Communist sympathizers across the Western world and the United Nations. They escalated their efforts, forcing the Air Force to respond in kind. The world press condemned the raids with feigned indignation. Yet MACV had no choice but to punish the invaders lest the aggression resulted in greater loss of American lives.

On this day, an Arc Light mission was being flown along the Fish Hook area of Cambodia. It was a dense jungle region extending from the plains of Mimot near the northeastern Vietnamese border to the mountainous terrain of O'Rang where the Sihanouk Trail and the Ho Chi Minh Trail intersected. It was here where COSVAN (*Central Office For South Vietnam), the VC political and military headquarters, resided.

The commander of the lead B-52 of Hickory Cell, one of twenty-four three-aircraft cells, gasped as his plane took a direct hit on its starboard side. The surface-to-air missile arched from the jungle and struck a lightning death blow. The emergency alerts lit up the cockpit as the crew prepared to evacuate. They knew the enemy would flood the area with troops upon seeing the Stratofortress plummeting, but knew they had no choice.

Their worst fears were realized as they drifted to the ground and found themselves surrounded by a pirate band of Khmer Rouge guerrillas. Many wore strips of cloth wrapped around stringy-haired, oval shaped heads. Some wore uniforms, though others were barebacked and wore sandals instead of boots. A large number were ex-convicts who bore the marks of the shackle and the lash. They set the pace with a brutal beatdown before hauling the Americans into captivity.

Up above, an OV-10 Bronco circled above the wreckage site. Its crew scanned the triple-canopied jungle area trying to make visual contact. Major Hinton's radio had been crushed beneath a Khmer bootheel, silenced to the chagrin of the recon crew. The Bronco hovered until targeted by anti-aircraft fire and reluctantly returned to base.

"You sure seem to have fallen hard for this girl."

"Yeah, I reckon, She's some kind of special."

Fritz missed Richard coming by for their coffee daybreak and came to inquire. He saw Richard engrossed in a letter from overseas as he sat at the stand before the Shanty. Richard handed him a studio pic of an exquisitely beautiful girl. On the back it was dedicated to Richard with love. It was signed by Laura.

"That's the one you met on that furlough we got," Fritz gave the photo back. "Guess you're not long for the Dark Side of the World."

"I wouldn't say that," Richard put the pic back in the envelope and slipped it into his robe pocket. "Still got a job to do."

"I haven't had a girlfriend since I earned my beanie," Fritz admitted. "I get my share of poontang, but I'm not looking to send some poor girl to Heartbreak Hotel."

"That's not what I've got in mind for Laura either."

"Don't think she'll take kindly to seeing you in a box."

"And who's gonna put either of us in one?" Richard scoffed.

"Nothing in that envelope about me. Besides, there's worse."

"Pray tell."

"Guys go back to the World every day in baskets with parts missing. Is that what you want for her? Can't get yourself up out of bed, can't make your way to the bathroom, barely able to feed yourself. Is that what she gets for her loyalty?"

"With all due respect, Fritz, your Mom married a war criminal. She had to leave her home, everything she knew, and moved to a remote place in a foreign land. I know she wouldn't have traded it for the world. Look at the son she was blessed with."

"There's my point. They were able to have a son."

"Look, if they blow your balls off you aren't gonna make it anyway. So that means there's still a sex life. As for the rest of it, well, what makes one different than a cat or a dog? They can't talk, can't feed themselves, can't clean up after themselves, can't take them anywhere. All they're good for is companionship. So what's the difference?"

"You've got your mind made up. And she is definitely worth the gamble, from what I see."

At length they saw Sgt. Tran of the LLDB coming down Path Five. He stopped and saluted at a respectable distance.

"I apologize for the intrusion. Captain Fred requests your attendance at a meeting at the Post in a half hour."

The twosome were unfashionably late as usual and had to take seats at the opposite ends of the adjoining luncheon tables where the A-Team awaited. There was a smattering of boos along with scowls from Fred and Jim before the meeting resumed.

"Okay, here's the deal," Fred informed them. "We had a couple of B-52s shot down during Operation Arc Light out by the Fish Hook in Cambodia. One landed near the border and we've got the Marines going in to pull the crew out. The other one's a problem. Recon's unable to establish radio contact. We had a local Montagnard CIDG (*Civilian Irregular Defense Group) platoon scour the area and there's no sign of them. We're thinking they got captured by the Khmer Rouge."

"We'll need one team to provide backup for the Marines in the area," Fred pointed to sites on a wall map. "The Special Forces team near Xuan Loc got pretty banged up in a firefight recently, so they gave us a call. The second team will be going in with the Montagnards and see if we can find out what happened to the MIA's."

"I guess Fritz and I'll go get the MIA's," Richard raised a finger. "A Khmer unit hauling around a dozen flyboys in jungle land in broad daylight shouldn't be hard to find."

"Well, that settles it, I guess," Fred said resignedly. He was vaguely uncomfortable with the same volunteers accepting all the risky assignments. Yet he could have accused of favoritism or bias if he had rejected the offers and instead placed others in harm's way. "You two get together with Jim and come up with a game plan. The rest of you saddle up, we'll have a plane here in an hour."

Jim got together with Richard and Fritz after the meeting adjourned and the rest of the team was headed back to Deadwood.

"I'm sure you two are familiar with the cardinal rule in the military," he shook his head. "Is there something I should know?"

"Well, we're not much for having to clean up after the jarheads, for one," Richard explained. "For another, we're making lots of progress working with the Yards. This sounds like it'll be a learning experience."

"Since you put it that way," Jim assented. "I know Richard's worked with the Rhade near Saigon. Fritz, you won't find them much different than the Bru. They may be more experienced with Army weapons, gear, strategy and tactics. They're much like the Bru as far as hunting, tracking and jungle skills go. They'll be able to see what you've learned from the Bru and they'll respect it."

They were flown from Dong Ha to Saigon, where they caught a helicopter ride to the Quan Loi Base Camp near the Cambodian border. There they met with a CIDG Montagnard squad composed of Rhade warriors. The leader was known as the Hawk, a middle-aged man who had fought the Communists since the French occupation after World War II. Richard identified himself as the Fox, Fritz as the Wolf, the names accorded them by the elders of the Bru.

"Okay, let's head out," Richard addressed the group, speaking Montagnard in his Missourian accent. "We'll ride the chopper out to the crash site and take the hike from there. We'll move quietly, move fast, and hit hard when we catch the bastards who wrecked our plane."

The Red Khmers had advanced beyond the American search perimeter with brutal efficacy. The platoon had set their captives on a forced march during which they gave no quarter. Some of the airmen had been injured so that their comrades were forced to help them along. Those who lagged were beaten with fists and rifle stocks. One aviator with a severe leg wound was carried by each arm by two teammates. They were at the end of the line, and caused the procession to halt as one of the airmen was tripped from behind. The Khmers laughed evilly as the wounded man landed face first onto the muddy ground.

"Fools!" Lieutenant Chan roared. "The path to the City is but ten kilometers away. You can have your sport once we are safely within."

He spoke of the Invisible City of the Red Khmers, a

legendary underground village located beneath a mountain in southeast Cambodia. The existence of the City was disputed though the Montagnards were well acquainted with its campaigns of violence and terror. They knew that when the prisoners entered its thresholds, they would never be seen again.

Chan was well known by MACV who had warrants out for his arrest. He was an ex-con recruited by the CIA at Long Binh Prison for duty with the A-Team at Gio Linh. He became the leader of their fledgling Provincial Reconnaisance Unit. Only he led them to defect to the Viet Cong once their training was completed. From there he eluded capture by the Americans by crossing into Cambodia and joining the Red Khmers. He led a massacre of a border village and was promoted to lieutenant thereafter. They were confident he could capture the downed B-52 crew and bring them to the City.

"Roy, these bastards'll kill us before we get to where we're headed," Lt. Scott hissed painfully. Five of the men were fettered together by cable wire, elbows and wrists tied agonizingly behind their backs.

"I should've never pulled my ripcord," Major Hinton managed before a guard threw a right cross that nearly cracked his jaw.

They continued through the steaming jungle until arriving at an open plain bordered by triple-canopied treelines. Beyond this could be seen a blue ridge of mountains, beneath which was the Invisible City of the Red Khmers.

"This is the last possible area of enemy concealment before we reach the plain," Chan announced. "Our strength of numbers will discourage any outside interference."

His worst fears were realized as his echoing words were drowned by the deafening roars on either side of the column. Eight Claymore mines were detonated on either side of the group as they came into range on the killing ground. His men were shredded by fragmentation before being sprayed by automatic fire. Chan and his troops returned fire at the smoking barrels in the treeline on both sides.

"Kill the prisoners!" Chan screamed. His men pulled their blades and began stabbing the necks of the fallen Americans. Only after the airmen had been slaughtered did the Khmers cease fire and toss their weapons aside.

They stared apprehensively as the ambush team emerged from both sides of the killing ground. The men were oval-skulled, black-skinned Montagnards, clad similarly to the Khmers. They were armed to the teeth with rifles at the ready.

"Perhaps there has been a mistake," Chan cleared his throat. "We are Popular Forces who captured these war criminals lying at our feet. We were bringing them to justice before you administered your own."

"You are heading west. Phnom Penh is to the north," the paramilitary leader scowled.

"We were bringing them to Kampot, where justice is swift and sure,"Chan said reassuringly.

"Kampot is a haven for thieves and murderers," the leader snarled. "The Viet Minh and the Red Khmers are the worst of the lot."

"Come now, brother, let us reason together." Chan grew condescending. "Certainly you do not fight for a cowardly Prince who sells our nation to the Americans as a harlot. It is clear and evident that you and your brave men have taken up arms in the name of the people. I have no doubt that we are united in the cause to liberate Cambodia in the common bond of justice and freedom."

"I can tell by your words that you are a Communist," the man spat on the ground. "We are Stieng Montagnards opposed to godless Communism. Cambodia will never be ruled by North Vietnam. Ever."

"Brother Dega," a fighter nodded toward the foliage behind them. Both teams bristled at the sight of two Americans stepping out at the fore of an armed group of Montagnard hunters.

"Perhaps I can make a suggestion."

"Who are you?"

"I am the Fox. I am with Special Forces at Dong Ha. I am escorted by the Hawk, who is a leader of the Rhade tribe. We came to rescue these soldiers who were murdered before your eyes. They were unarmed and accused by no one. We demand justice."

"So now the roles are reversed," said Dega. "These men were bringing the captives to justice before they took the law into their own hands."

"I can assure you they will receive justice," Richard smirked. "Turn them over to us and we will be on our way."

"What kind of justice?" a confederate spoke out. "Lowlander justice?"

"I can speak," the Hawk stepped up. "We are members of FULRO. Rest assured they will be brought to a place where our customs are honored."

"If they take us across the border, we will be persecuted as freedom fighting Cambodians," Chan bargained. "Take us to Phnom Penh if you must."

"This is bullshit," Fritz growled in English. "We can take them by force."

"I'm not sure if you noticed we're kinda outnumbered," Richard said softly.

"And when's that been a problem?"

"Hear the dogs barking in their crude language," Chan insisted. "I can guarantee you they are planning a deception.

The white man will plunge a knife in your back without a thought. It is their way of life."

"Say," Fritz turned to an interpreter, who carried an English-Cambodian dictionary. "How do you say 'go screw yourself'?"

"It is as you say," Dega noted. "The Prince is weak and fearful of the Communists. You have killed unarmed men on our hunting grounds. Their spirits will find no rest. We will take you to our elders and they will decide."

"This is not good," one of the Khmers sidled over to Chan as they were led into the jungle toward the village. "We have conducted more than a few operations in this area. If any of the savages recognize us, it may cause a problem."

"Not so much," Chan regained his confidence. "What shall they prove us with? Mugshots? Arrest files? These ones who are taking us are not so far removed from civilization. Their consciences will have them bring us elsewhere."

The Stieng village was located two miles above sea level on a plateau overlooking the nearby valley. Although they had been plundered by their enemies, they were showing signs of recovery. A cow was giving milk, and two calves were feeding in the distance. An ox was plowing the field, and a dozen chickens fluttered behind a fenceline. Vegetables began to sprout where farmers tilled the watered soil.

The villagers slowly gathered as the warriors led the strangers into the village. Women, children and the elderly stared in wonder at the Americans. Most had never seen a white man in their lives. Only they saw the hard-looking Rhade and realized there was a dispute. Yet it was the sight of the lowland Cambodians that caused the most consternation. The tension flared as an old woman cried in terror at the sight of the guerrillas. An old man wept in horror, covering his eyes as he fled from the scene.

"Doesn't look good for you, chickenshit," Fritz sidled up to Chan.

"We shall see, white pig," Chan snarled back.

The strangers were ushered to a great warehouse that also served as the town hall. Everyone in the village arrived save for the elderly man and woman who recoiled at the sight of the guerrillas. The Cambodians and the Rhade were set apart at the front of the room, and everyone awaited the arrival of the village elders. At length, five little old men entered the meeting and seats were brought for them as the proceedings began.

"I have been approached by many wishing to give their testimony," the tribal chief Anak spoke, "All shall be heard as we seek justice in this matter."

"Old man, justice has been served today," Chan tried to remain calm. "The murderers who bring death from above have received their own portion. We have given them their eternal reward in the name of the Cambodian people. All we ask now is to return to our place to continue our crusade for liberty and justice."

"Are we on *Candid Camera* here?" Fritz looked around the warehouse.

"Dammit, will you chill out," Richard whispered.

"There are some among our families who claim to recognize your men," Anak held a hand toward the crowd surrounding the place of judgment. "Let them speak now."

One by one the villagers stepped forth and confronted the guerrillas. A widow wept bitterly as she related how her daughter went to pick fruit and never returned. She went searching and saw Chan and his men leaving the mountainside. Hours later a hunting party found the girl's body at the bottom of a ravine. She had been raped and murdered.

Her neighbors were both outraged and inspired as they spoke out. They told of incidents during which their fences had been toppled and their cattle rustled by the Red Khmers. Others detailed how their chickens were stolen along with baskets of produce. Chan seethed as the villagers continued to denounce his men. Finally a little boy was allowed to testify.

"I hate those men!" he cried. "They killed my dog."

"Can you describe what happened? Tell us of it."

"He was fluffy and cuddly," the boy sobbed.

He was lifted over the shoulder of a hunter and carried kicking and screaming from the room.

"This is absurd," Chan was indignant. "Our soldiers are defending our nation from the white marauders and you deny us a couple of eggs and some vegetables. Even more ridiculous is to suggest one of your cows accompanied us down the mountain."

"O wise one," the Hawk beseeched. "We are not here to seek retribution for the theft of livestock, or even the killing of a domestic animal. These men have killed a child and are suspected in the disappearance of others. Moreover, we saw them butcher twelve men before our eyes. As it is written, the blood of the innocent demands blood atonement. Also, the sacredness of life is profaned by the murderer, whose sins must never go unpunished."

"You savage!" Chan bellowed. "You take the side of these white bastards. You take pity on a child weeping over a mangy cur. Who will take your side or weep for you when our comrades come to avenge this insult?"

"Your very words condemn you," Anak passed judgment. "You call our people savages, yet it is you who bring savagery to our land."

"I hate to interrupt, but we're running the meter here,"

Richard spoke out. "Let us take these scumbags outside and get this over with."

"A life for a life," the Hawk was adamant. "Our tradition demands it."

"We have no law to put a man to death," Anak determined. "This is a decision only a priest can make."

"You have no idea what bloodshed and destruction you are bringing down upon your village by this mindlessness," Chan exclaimed, turning to the emotion-filled witnesses. "You speak of retribution. If a hair on our heads is harmed, it will be on your loved ones when the ministers of justice come to call."

"His words stand as evidence against him," Anak turned to his fellow elders, who nodded in assent. "Let them be brought before the priest. We must wash our hands of their fate."

And so the hunters brought the guerrillas along a path to the mountainside. At length they approached a cavern shielded from view by a treeline that gave way to a cobblestone clearing. The Americans and the Rhade followed closely, with the villagers not far behind. Only Richard and Fritz were taken aback as many knelt on the pavement, some banging their heads against the stones.

This was the Temple of Xo.

The procession made its way across a pool of black marble upon which sat a pyramid rising twenty steps of granite above the floor. At its apex was an obsidian block inscribed with arcane symbols and writings. Behind it sat a small golden throne, and to its rear was a golden statue of Xo. The triple-headed deity rose ten feet above the dais, its heads representing truth, liberty and justice. Its faces glared with righteous indignation, angered by the inadequacies of its followers.

From the candle-lit darkness shuffled a dwarfish man who painstakingly made his way down the steps to meet his visitors. He appeared as a turkey dressed in silken robes of orange and red, as a blazing sunrise. His torso was round, his spindly limbs seeming as if they might fail at any moment. His oval skull sat on an impossibly slender neck, his eyes covered by cauls that were as those of a stillborn infant.

"O men, what causes you to muster the courage to come into the presence of almighty Xo without warrant?" the ancient seer inquired.

"Wise priest, we come to you for guidance," the Hawk genuflected before him. "We come to the temple for truth and justice according to our tradition. Here stands before you a band of men accused of theft, robbery and murder. They have sinned greatly against the peace of our land and the commandments of Xo. We have no law that allows for the prosecution of such men so that their punishment can fit their crimes."

"Rhade bastard," Chan cried out. "I will send your mothers and daughters to whorehouses, and the rest of your villages will consider them blessed with what is in store."

"You see, O great one," Hawk concluded. "He confesses his violence and reveals his true nature."

"I know no shame!" Chan roared. "We slaughtered men the color of scum. The crimes you accuse us of is the just tribute we ask as protectors of your realm. If that gilded monstrosity above us is your reason to live, let your men join our battle so you may find true dignity in death. Bless our efforts and join our cause."

"Ai!" the priest screamed, tearing his robes at the blasphemy. "Ai! Never have such words been spoken in this hallowed place. Though such a price has not been demanded in many moons, these crimes and this heresy must be repaid. Prepare these men to meet the great and terrible Xo."

"You know, if this white devil stuff catches on, we may have some major problems getting out of here," Fritz pulled a tiny vial from his pocket and handed it to Richard. Inside were two small tabs.

"What? A trip?" Richard recognized the LSD-coated paper tablets.

"I dropped a tab of THC when we got into this mess. It's starting to wear off. Figure we might as well enjoy the show."

"Ah, what the heck," Richard said. "I was wondering how you got so mouthy."

He licked the tip of his finger, picked up a tab and put it in his mouth. Fritz took the second one and put the vial away.

The events that followed were surreal so as not to require mind-altering substances in making witnesses doubt their sanity. The hunters bound the wrists and blindfolded the accused before lining them up at the left side of the pyramid. One by one they were led up the steps to the top level where the priest awaited. The hunters were instructed to force the men to a kneeling position before the obsidian block. They were then pushed down with their chests upon it.

The priest uttered guttural chants and demonic oaths as he wielded a gold-bladed sword that was almost his equal in height. As the unrepentant was pressed down on the block, the priest swung the blade so that the bandit's head was severed from the neck. The corpse convulsed as the head bounced down the steps, landing on the onyx floor with a meaty thud.

At length the bastard children of the village converged at the entrance to the temple. Their parents had wandered from the mountain on different days and times and never returned. According to tradition, the villagers erected huts for them and provided food and drink. The whelps of their hunting dogs were sometimes given for companionship. The children also learned they could come to the temple where the priest would give them scraps from the offerings to Xo.

They and their dogs crept to the foot of the pyramid and

availed themselves of the scraps as they were accustomed. They sat cross-legged on the floor and munched on the entrails of the severed heads, holding them as gourds. The dogs lapped up the blood that flowed as rivulets down the steps to form great puddles on the floor. Many of the women fled from the scene to avoid vomiting on the temple floor in revulsion.

Chan was the last to be executed. Richard had read that the beheaded of the French Revolution were able to see and hear for moments after their decapitation, according to scientific data. With that knowledge he picked up Chan's head by the hair.

"There, you shit bird," Richard stared at Chan's fluttering eyes. "I hope there's twelve pissed-off airmen awaiting before you get to where you're going."

With that he tossed Chan's head across the floor as a bowling ball. The hunters began collecting the heads and the bodies as the villagers chased the dogs and bastards away.

"Now, that was intense," Fritz said as they followed the villagers in departing from the temple.

"Yeah, I guess. What was that, anyway?"

"Purple Haze. I copped it off a gunner from Air Cav. Says he got it in Saigon."

"Last time I tripped, I had Sunshine. But this wasn't bad."

They followed the Rhade warriors into the jungle as the full moon rose overhead.

8

THE SIEGE

Richard Mc Cain woke one morning and saw a white-robed figure sitting by the window at the Shanty. The sun was rising and the pale light shone on who appeared to be his great-grandfather, Henry Geronimo.

"Do you think you are going to win this war?" the apparition asked.

"Hell yeah," Richard managed as if in a dream-like state. "Last time we met, you asked me to do you proud. Reckon I've done just that."

"There were many men of honor who fought in losing battles throughout history. Those who served under Napoleon, Bismarck, Howe, Robert E. Lee."

"We're not losing here," Richard was fervent. "We're fighting for truth, liberty and justice. We've invested too much. The Vietnamese people's lives are at stake."

"That is what they told you. Is that what you believe?"

"That's why I'm here. That's why we're here."

"Have you wondered why you have been drawn toward the mountain people? You see how they differ from the city folk.

Which group is more at peace? Whose lives have been changed by war?"

"Let me ask you," Richard narrowed his eyes at the vision. "They're no different than the natives on the reservations back home. The Indians in the cities get education, jobs, homes, a good life. Same with the people in Saigon. When people withdraw from society, their families suffer."

"When they embrace war, who suffers? Have you embraced war? Do you like killing?"

At that, Richard's soul was filled with turmoil. He only began to recover as he heard the soft pounding on the front door of the Shanty.

"Hey, whuzup?"

"Having a bad dream?" Fritz asked as Richard stepped aside and bade him enter. "Sounded like you were having a one-sided argument."

"Yeah, I was having a dream about my great-grandfather again."

"This place'll do that to you," Fritz peered around the candlelit shack. "You make coffee?"

"Nah. I got a neighbor who usually invites me by."

"Humph," Fritz pushed his black cloak back and took a seat on the sofa. "Tran came by. Fred wants us down in an hour for another meeting."

"So what's new?"

"Hey," Fritz crinkled his eyes at Richard after thanking him for a beer. "You okay?"

"He asked me if I liked killing," Richard popped the top on the can of Guinness and took a swig.

"Well," Fritz shrugged, "that's like asking a firefighter if he likes running into burning buildings. You do it because you can, because you're good at it. You save lives."

"Do you ever have weird dreams?"

"Uh…yeah," Fritz was non-committal.

"Sometimes I think it's the drugs. Sometimes I think it's this place. Like that whacked-out stuff that happened at the Temple."

"You're probably right."

"You know we never really talked about Zombie Night."

"We said we weren't gonna talk about it, remember?" Fritz cocked an eyebrow. "There's a line between tripping out and being considered for a Section Eight."

"Hey," Richard reasoned. "If they haven't put Bobby Cuddahy up for one, I doubt anyone goes."

"It follows you for the rest of your life, like a dishonorable discharge," Fritz insisted. "You think I don't have dreams? I remember stories my Dad told me. He didn't tell me war stories until I enlisted. That was when he wanted to give me a small idea of what to expect. Only we ended up opening a can of worms. It's one thing going after the bad guys for war crimes. It's another having to stand by and watch your comrades committing them."

"You're not talking about stuff we've done."

"No, that was payback. There's lots of villages getting burned just because Charlie goes in and robs their food. They call it aiding and abetting. Men stand up to defend their homes and they get their heads caved in. You've heard stories, so have I. We get pissed off until we see some teenager from New Jersey carried off the field with his legs blown off. That changes our perspective. We just have to take care that our vision doesn't get blurred so we can't see the line anymore."

"To think we signed up for this crap," Richard shook his head.

"Well, we'd best show up early for the meeting," Fritz chugged the beer and crushed the can. "I'm not in the mood for catching crap for being late."

. . .

Fred and Jim were somber as usual when the meeting commenced. Their standard procedure was to hold a radioed discussion with MACV/SOG in Saigon for the latest news before passing the info along to the team. There were rarely any uplifting tidbits to pass along, especially when the meetings were called the first thing in the morning.

"Okay, guys, it looks like Victor Charles is up to his old tricks," Fred opened the meeting. "Word has it that he's making another run at our position. He's specifically making a move on our neighbors at the Combat Base, but we know we're gonna get all the spillover."

"Question," Fritz could not help himself. "How can you smoke those things so early in the morning?"

"Same way you guys wake up and open a can of beer," Fred glowered. "Now knock it off. We think he's going with his three-pronged attack as usual. Main force driving hard up the middle, skirmish lines east and west going for the bracket. He may be planning something new in crossing the Minefield. There's been lots of desertions over the VC assigning units to the suicide squad. Now the story is that they've got ways to cross over safely. We don't know what they've got in mind but we're gonna find out."

"Okay, our assignments," Jim stepped up in front of the map of the base camp. "I'll be working the northwest sector along with the Montagnard warriors. We'll be defending our left flank and holding the high ground against a possible sweep around the Minefield. Fred will be directing traffic at the northeast sector. The LLDB will lead the RFPF counterattack against any sweeping moves. Our A-Team will act as reinforcement and support as necessary. Fritz and Richard will be in charge of the CIDG reinforcements rolling in from

Saigon this afternoon. They will hold down our fortifications in front of the camp and keep us from being overrun."

"This is just great," Jerry Brown rolled his eyes. "We get the Low Life Dick Brains leading the Ruff and Puffs' desperate struggle to keep the Good Ol' White Boys from getting their asses stomped."

"Should work out just fine for you," Jim could not help himself. "You're the shiniest white boy in town."

"Hey, screw you, Red Man," the albino leaped to his feet and was restrained by Al and Charlie. "Everybody knows your agenda. You sit up on the ledge smoking the peace pipe with the savages while the rest of us are down here fighting off sappers every night. The VC don't give a crap about overrunning your swamp. They're coming at us, and your bows and arrows don't fly this far."

The tension in the air curdled the room. There had been a rivalry between Jim and Jerry, considered the senior member of the team. Fred was weighing his words before Richard interceded.

"Everybody knows about the piece of work Fritz and I did with the Yards in Cambodia last week," Richard spoke softly. "I can speak for the Yards. They are tough, courageous and loyal. We wouldn't be standing here if it weren't for them. I can assure you they won't stand by and watch if we're being overrun. They'll take a hand way before that starts to happen. And if you guys get hit too hard at your position, either Fritz or I will pull some of our cidgees loose and lend a hand."

"Yeah, well," Jerry conceded. "So how big of a dinner party are we expecting? Another division?"

"You know the drill," Fritz smiled wryly. "The bigger they are, the harder they'll fall."

The team rose and exchanged handshakes before retiring to

their positions in preparing for one of the biggest fights of their careers.

It was 0300 when the bugles began echoing in the darkness beyond the Minefield in a bizarre parody of reveille. The VC used bugles and whistles as field communication in directing traffic between squads, platoons and companies. Most of the Green Berets were high-tension wired and needed no call to action. Some could not sleep, others resorted to amphetamines. Only Luke Sanderson and Bobby Cuddahy slept soundly as babes and had to be roused for the fight. Luke spent his youth guarding moonshine stills in the hills of Kentucky. He would allow US Treasury agents to wake him at risk of a shotgun blast. He regarded the VC as no different.

The A-Team was equipped with high-tech Starlight scopes that allowed them to identify targets at three hundred yards. Only when they spotted enemy movement, they asked their CIDG riflemen with binoculars to verify what they were seeing. The volunteers were equally uncertain as to what they were sighting. Soon Captain Federer had to return to the Post for aerial confirmation.

"We're having some technical difficulties out by the DMZ," an Air Force officer in Saigon explained. "We won't be able to provide support until the issues are resolved."

"What are you talking about?" there was a cloud of smoke above Fred's head. "My guys are spotting heavy troop movement. We're talking companies taking positions along the treelines. Last time we got hit we were outnumbered three to one. This looks worse. Request immediate air recon, and I want this escalated ASAP."

"Having to put this on hold, Captain," the officer was

apologetic. "We're trying to identify and classify. We've got unidentified aircraft in the area moving at questionable speed in uncertain flight patterns. We know they're not North Vietnamese. The concern is whether they're Chinese or Russian. We can't send in air support until we know what we're up against."

"What the hell are you talking about? You been watching too much TV? Lemme speak to your superior officer."

"I regret to inform you I rank you, Captain. This is Major Ethan Hunt. The officer-in-command is in triage with the CIA and the Pentagon. Right now we're assessing the situation. If whatever it is can outmaneuver our Phantom jets, our B-52's will lack adequate protection. We've already had a couple taken out recently. We can't afford to take any more forty million-dollar losses."

"And what are my men's lives worth?" Fred lost it. "Fuck you!"

"Say again?"

Fred threw the headphone at the communication console aside and stalked out of the Post with Steve Korn at his side.

"What's up, skipper? Is it a no-go?"

"I know that drug use is rampant here, but this is too much."

"What do you mean?"

"Those nincompoops are telling me they're seeing flying saucers out here. How am I supposed to relay that to the team?"

"I can handle it," Steve was ebullient as always. "I'm a Trekkie going back to the beginning. You know, a *Star Trek* fan. I got heavily into UFO research, I'm all about Roswell and Area 51. I can explain everything in detail."

"Now why isn't that making me feel glad all over?" Fred growled as he lit a fresh cigar and trudged up Path Four to the battle in progress.

Everyone's a superhero, everyone's a Captain Kirk.

GERMAN ROCK SONG

"Okay, this is starting to make no sense," Richard said as he and Fritz swiped binoculars and Starlight scopes from the Montagnards trying to relay their findings. "I thought the gooks were using spotlights. Only why in hell would they have the spotlights going back and forth like that? Thing is, if they have aircraft with that capability, why haven't they fired a shot yet?"

"Why are the white leaders not sending their great guns and aircraft to destroy this enemy?" the Hawk wondered. He had been dispatched along with a Rhade CIDG platoon to join the fray.

"With all due respect," Fritz spoke the Rhade dialect with a Germanic accent, "you couldn't hit one of them if they were ten feet in front of you."

"Perhaps the Viet Minh have found a way to conjure up devils," the Hawk mused. "Possibly we are fighting demons."

"Just what I needed to hear," Fritz rolled his eyes.

"This is a diversionary tactic," Richard decided. "The dinks are figuring we'll be looking at the sky when they come across. The only thing that'll be looking up will be their heads lying in the mud. Let's get to it, boys."

The group awaited as the VC began their monstrous procession. Squads of twelve approached the minefield with mats and mattresses which absorbed the detonation of landmines. There was great loss as the guerrillas were ripped to shreds by the mines they tread upon. Yet it gave way to their comrades who surged forth in their goal of breaching the Americans' defenses.

Once again the Green Berets gave orders to have the M-60 machine guns brought to the fore. They were fed by 100-round belts that were often left in the ammunition boxes for easier and quicker handling. The gunners would shoot low to high, hoping to score head shots on crouching soldiers, take out the legs of advancing soldiers, and rip the torsos of those taking the knee to aim and fire back. The withering fire cost the enemy as great of a loss as the mines, Yet they persisted.

"I've got them coming in around a hundred yards from the fenceline," Richard radioed Fred as he focused his binoculars on the approaching insurgents. "We got anything on our air support yet?"

"They don't have a make on the unidentified aircraft yet," Fred's voice was garbled by static. "Play defense, conserve your ammo, look for opportunities to outflank them away from the fenceline. If we can buy a couple of hours we regain the advantage when the sun comes up."

"Tell me something I don't know, skipper. Fox out."

"Eagle to Fox," Jim's voice came in on the radio.

"Well, well. Another ham operator."

"Too bad we're not in a convoy heading south. Listen, I've got your flank. I've got a platoon of warriors up here on the ledge and we're getting good distance with our arrow volleys. Lots of Charlies going down and not getting back up."

"Good thing they're not using up ammo. We're gonna be light down here in a couple of hours. We'll be cutting it close."

"Like George Washington once said, wait until you see the whites of their eyes."

"Like hell," Richard chuckled. "Fox out."

There was sporadic fire as the VC formed defensive clusters around torn chunks of barricades from where they could regroup. They had attempted to breach Dogpatch but that was the area of greatest resistance. The residents had been given firearms and were taking shots at targets in the distance where movement was lively. They had also been instructed to conserve ammo. Only those who had taken rifle practice with the LLDB were encouraged to fire upon distant targets.

"Wolf to Fox."

"Yeah, Earth to Roger Ramjet. Whuzup?"

"I'm pretty sure I'm scoring head shots on fire teams out there," he replied. His statement was punctuated by a report that echoed across the clearing and repeated through the walkie-talkie. "Kinda hard not to cut some extra rounds loose when you see them in a group."

"How you holding out?"

"I probably have about ten magazines left. When I run out I'll probably start collecting extras from the ruff and puffs. Don't really wanna do that."

"Copy that."

The kneejerk reaction would be that the white men were taking their ammo out of self-preservation, leaving the natives defenseless. Only few realized that the Green Berets were decorated marksmen who made every shot count.

"Lion to Fox."

"Lion?" Richard chuckled. "Where'd you get that?"

"From a Cracker Jack box, same as you," Fred replied. "We've mustered up about a dozen mortar rounds. It's not air and arty (*artillery), but it's better than nothing. We're seeing heavy movement shifting toward the middle of the field on your end. We're gonna let 'er rip and hope it helps."

"You're the skipper," Richard concurred. "Have at it."

There was a long pregnant silence before a series of loud thumps resonated from the distance outside Dogpatch. A short interval gave way to mighty explosions that clustered about eighty yards in the distance. The team had been concerned about intermittent whistles emanating from the sector. After the blasts, they strained to hear if there was anything in response to the mortar volley. Only silence covered the land.

Yet within minutes, a cacophany of bugle blares both startled and discouraged the defenders as it drifted across the west end of the field.

"They're just screwing with our heads," Richard blurted into the receiver. "They're trying to make us think we missed our target. I'm thinking the dumbasses are giving away their location. Request permission to split my force. I'm going over the fence to do recon, see what they got left on my right flank."

"That's a negative, Sergeant," Fred was adamant. "Hold your position until we can do a damage assessment. If they dug in and weathered the storm you may be walking into a trap. We're still taking sniper fire on our end. We've taken ARVN casualties and a couple of guys from the team got hit. No fatalities."

"I'm with Uncle Fred on that," Fritz chimed in. "No sense in risking exposure. I'm figuring they're closing in on the seventy-yard line. They still got a long way to go."

"We still got Claymores out there that haven't been popped yet," Richard replied.

"You can still see they haven't touched the concertina wire out that way. Most likely the forward units carrying the cushions backed off from the mortar rounds. It bought us time," Fritz assessed.

"I'm going off the air for the next half hour," Fred announced. "I'm calling HQ for a support update. I'll be damned if the gyrene base is going off like Fourth of July and I can't get a few boxes of reloads."

. . .

Fred and Steve trudged back up the slope to the Post where they took seats at the command console and contacted Saigon for guidance. Instead they got a static-filled transmission from nearby.

"Hellboy to Lion. Base One asked me to let you know I'm flying the friendly skies above your location waiting for the green light."

"Green light?" Fred's cigar fumed. "I'm almost out of mortar rounds. My team is scraping the bottom of the barrel for machine gun ammo. Charlie's already plowed our field, he's gonna have an open road to our fenceline if he gets inside our fifty-yard line. Don't tell me you're running out of napalm."

"Not the problem," Hellboy replied. "There's something here from somewhere else. We got a cell of three unidentified aircraft buzzing the perimeter. They're at the DMZ, I can't take them out without justifiable cause."

"At the DMZ? I had this thrown at me an hour ago. Are they just sitting there?"

"Roger that. Up there flitting around like lightning bugs. I try and line them up in my sights and they bounce away like laser beams. I need to get clearance from the Pentagon to engage. CIA's even looking into it. There's two more of us out here. When we get indication we're gonna put some lights out."

"Rhino to Wolf," Fritz heard Chuck Valentine's voice.

"Go ahead."

"Update on our supply situation. We're gonna make the ultimate sacrifice. We're having the RFPF's bring out our liquor supply for conversion to Molotov cocktails."

"Damn it to hell," Fritz scowled. "I certainly hope you're doing that as a last resort."

"That's a ten-four. We've still got a box of grenades left, but after that we're flat out. The mortars are all gone."

"You're not gonna get a lot of throwing distance with the Molotovs. Suggest you pour them out into smaller units."

"Way ahead of you. The puffs are rounding up every glass bottle they can find. If we pour the good stuff out and Arc Lights come through at the last minute, we'll be drinking out of soda bottles this summer."

"Fox to Rhino," Richard cut in.

"Go ahead."

"We're doing the same thing with gasoline and propane. Gas is going into small cans, propane getting set on wagons. Not placing much stock on the cidgees' throwing skills. We'll set them out at strategic positions if the enemy gets inside the fifty."

"No Willie McCovey on our team. We'll wait until the VC are climbing the fence, and we'll bounce the bottles off their heads."

"Sounds like a plan."

Within a half hour, Richard and Fritz got the harrowing call from Jim.

"Bad news. We're seeing movement at the fifty. I'm gonna put my team in position. We're gonna send a flurry from the ledge, then we'll go down and look for quality shots. I've got a squad of cidgee riflemen, but everyone else carries bows and arrows. And it's not like they're gonna resupply our arrows."

"Be careful, Grandpa," Fritz said softly. "We can't lose you."

He made his way over to where Richard was hunkered down alongside the Hawk at a concrete bunker sitting five yards behind a brick and mortar portion of the fenceline.

"I got movement at the fifty. Grandpa was right. Looks like fire teams, maybe squads, nothing we can't handle. I can't figure out why they're not signaling a full frontal. We'll have daylight in a couple of hours. Charlie has to have lost a couple hundred already. He can't cut his losses just like that."

To the team's delight, they saw a heavy volley of arrows arching across the sky and landing along the markers delineating the fifty-yard line. The secondary movements indicated a large number hit their targets.

"*Gott im himmel!*" Fritz crowed, slapping palms with Richard and the Hawk. "*Sieg heil! Heil Opa!*"

"I can go with all that," Richard chuckled, peering through his binoculars. To his consternation, mats were being tossed over the row of concertina wire at the fifty as over a dozen bodies were being carried away.

"They're still coming," Fritz looked down his Starlight scope. He took a pot shot at a silhouette in the distance and grunted in satisfaction as a scarlet cloud exploded behind its head. "At least they're in decent range. I still say we should have the cidgees hold their fire until they get to the twenty."

"That's cutting it close," Richard grimaced. "Okay, let's try this. I'm going with the Hawk and his platoon, we'll try a right sweep. Tell Fred we're moving out so we don't take any friendly fire. If you see us going hand-to-hand, that'll mean either we got ambushed or we're out of ammo. Maybe you can free up the Crazy Eight and send them along."

"Hell," Fritz scoffed. "I'll be leading the charge."

And so Richard and the Hawk guided the Montagnards through a gateway along the fenceline. They continued toward a subtly marked path that led toward the concertina at the twenty-five yard marking. Richard found the narrow aperture separating the concertina and rows of spiked bamboo that led to yet another trapless lane.

They approached the barricade at the fifty-yard line and could see the VC bringing up mats that they launched over the coiled rolls of barbed wire. Their comrades assumed firing positions, watching the fenceline for signs of activity as they completed draping the barricade with ten mats, side by side. It would facilitate their move in hurtling the concertina and taking cover to prepare for their next charge.

"Hey, Charlie," they heard a voice calling in Vietnamese with a Missourian accent. "Looks like you missed a spot."

The VC were startled by the sound and were slow to react as a flurry of arrows whizzed through the air. There were two squads of twelve riflemen, and eight of them fell to the ground with shafts protruding from their heads, necks and torsos. Richard's squad followed his lead in charging into their midst with steel blades thrashing. He knew that they would not be able to fire their rifles at close range for fear of hitting their comrades. It allowed him to wield his machete as a farmer clearing a field of chaff.

The Missourian was as a giant among pygmies in slaughtering enemy. His sinewy six-foot, 210-pound frame bobbed and weaved as he sliced his way through the VC, who stood 5'4" and weighed 120 pounds on average. He severed arms and hands, slicing through necks and cleaving skulls. The Montagnards were skilled knife fighters who were adept at ripping torsos from collarbone to navel just as they gutted the carcasses of wild game. Within minutes the attack was over. Richard and the Hawk rallied the warriors, some of whom had suffered minor injuries at best.

At once they heard the blaring of bugles and piercing whistles as the enemy began to rally. Their leaders saw the skirmish along the barricade and the opportunity that lay ahead. They exhorted their squads to advance to the mat-covered concertina and begin the charge that might well take them to the fenceline and victory.

"Ho, dogs!" Richard roared, his upper body dripping with the blood and gore spilled by the vanquished. "Let us retreat to the fence and make sure we're not followed before we get to cover. Otherwise we defend the line at all costs. Don't forget we're the only thing separating the Communists from the women and children on base."

Richard and the Hawk signaled the retreat as they ducked back behind the concertina and rushed along the clearing back to the fenceline. They relied on fire and movement, two four-man fire teams spreading out in kneeling positions and laying down cover as their teammates doubled back for ten yards. They then provided cover as the first group retreated. Richard cursed and swore as an enemy round ripped the skull of one of the warriors. The native fell face first, his brains splattering the ground before him.

They made it to the fenceline and realized a platoon of VC were in pursuit. Their numbers dwindled as they stumbled across the minefield and were ripped asunder. Yet a large portion of their number remained when they caught up with Richard's group. The defenders were out of ammo and had no choice but to charge their pursuers with their blades.

The attackers smelled victory, only they were caught off-guard once again as a flurry of arrows cascaded down upon their ranks. They heard war whoops and cries as Jim Tate led the charge of his warriors from the west flank. Richard felt as if the odds were in their favor despite the fact their backs were literally against the wall.

He swung his blade with such force that his opponent's head rolled from his shoulders, blood spurting from his neck. He confronted a guerrilla trying to gain his feet, and in doing so the man pulled his firearm and aimed it at Richard's face.

Richard tried to roll but there was a gunshot. Richard saw Fritz Hammer leaping through the air, blocking the shot before rolling to the ground. He looked at the fallen guerrilla, a knife protruding from his forehead.

"Dammit, Fritz, you saved my life," Richard dropped to his side. He saw blood pouring copiously from a left thigh wound.

"Yeah, well, I hope you can return the favor," Fritz snickered, nodding at the field. Richard looked out and nearly broke a cold sweat at the sight of hundreds of little men massing along the outer perimeter of the Minefield at the hundred-yard marker.

"Jim, what the hell is that?" Richard asked. The massive Indian's face was adorned with the war paint of the native Cheyenne, his bare torso streaked with the blood of enemy.

"Whatever it is, it don't look good," Jim peered out at the sea of humanity. "I told Fred I was going out, he had no complaints. I think they're getting hit pretty hard on his side. This might be Waterloo and the Alamo rolled into one unless the cavalry flies in."

Richard, Jim and the Hawk assisted the others in helping the wounded retreat behind the fenceline. Four of the warriors had been killed, yet there was no choice but to leave the bodies entangled in the carpet of dead obscured by the moonlit night. They only hoped that they themselves would not be counted among the dead if this next swarm succeeded in overrunning the camp.

"What're we gonna do, Fred?" Jim radioed as he stared out at the hundreds of oval-skulled men. He thought it odd that they were all shaven bald and not one wore as much as a bandana. They also went shirtless, nary a man wearing a uniform. It also seemed impossible that they carried no weapons, but that was too much to hope for.

"Hold your fire," Fred replied. "We're almost out over here.

I got men needing medical attention we can't afford to give. We'll be tossing free alcohol when they make their next move."

"You sit tight, brother," Jim assured him. "The Great Spirit's got us, I know it."

The words no sooner left his lips before the unthinkable happened.

At once a great vessel appeared from nowhere. It was as a gargantuan disc that descended upon a column of light which slowly began to surge from beneath. It began pulsating until, at once, a great flash of blinding energy exploded across the field as a nuclear blast. The defenders were forced to shield their eyes from the sight. Yet as soon as they were able to refocus, the field was again shrouded in darkness of night. The vessel, the lights and the legion of beings had disappeared into thin air.

"Friends of yours?" Fritz said weakly, pulling at a strip of cloth that was as a tourniquet around his thigh.

"They are the Plejaran," the Hawk said, staring in awe of the deserted field.

"The *what*?" Richard squinted, kneeling by Fritz and daubing his wound.

"I have heard the name spoken among the Cheyenne," Jim nodded.

"They are the race beyond the mountains," the Hawk had a strange look in his eye as if he had glimpsed into the netherworld. "They have existed since before the dawn of man. They are as watchers observing the ways of mankind. They are forbidden by the gods to meddle in our affairs. Yet they will make their presence known when they wish to distract men from engineering the destruction of their species and their land."

The team would learn much later that the Pentagon had authorized the scrambling of a cell of B-52's, one of which was armed with a nuclear weapon. A fleet of Phantom jets were on standby, ready to attack if the UFO's launched an attack on the bases surrounding Dong Ha. The general staff at MACV were greatly relieved when they received confirmation that they would not drop the third nuclear bomb in world history.

"Enough of this hocus-pocus crap," Fritz insisted as he was loaded onto a stretcher. "I think I'm ready for a shot of cognac."

"So am I, brother," Richard squeezed his shoulder. "So am I."

9

THE CHINK

And no marvel, for the Devil himself is transformed into an angel of light.

2 CORINTHIANS 11:14

The quote from Scripture headlined the mimeographed sheet which gave a one-page report of facts and figures about UFO's provided by Sgt. Steve Korn. It was a well-thought piece of research at first glance. Only it was never given a second thought as evidenced by nearly a dozen copies wadded into a ball and dropped into a trashcan outside the command trailer at the Post. Richard Mc Cain folded his and tucked it into his hip pocket as he arrived at the morning meeting. Fritz Hammer arrived earlier as Y Bro came to the Castle in a golf cart to give him a ride.

There was another pack of mimeographed sheets being distributed at the get-together, and they were being received with far greater interest in providing the team with high amusement.

WANTED
Richard Mc Cain --- Fritz Hammer
$10,000 REWARD

For war crimes and crimes against humanity as defined
by the Geneva Convention and atrocities against the Vietnamese
people and the government of the Democratic Republic of Vietnam.

Mc Cain is from Missouri USA and Hammer is from North
Dakota USA. They are both fluent in Vietnamese, Cambodian and
Montagnard dialects though fundamentally illiterate. They have
committed crimes of murder, robbery, burglary, arson, extortion,
blackmarketing, sabotage, and desecration of religious sites.

Both men are armed and extremely dangerous. They are wanted
dead or alive, Any information leading to their capture will be rewarded.

Report any and all sightings to the nearest representative or unit of the
National Liberation Front of South Vietnam.

"Damn," Chuck Valentine shook his head as he tossed the flyer onto the table where he sat. "You two are a couple of ugly mofos."

"Whoever drew those pictures had some sense of humor," Fritz retorted. The flyer included artist's sketches of the Americans at the top of the page. "You better watch it, Chuck. Somebody's liable to bring you in by mistake."

"Is that ten grand for both or separately?" Jerry Brown furrowed his brow. "I can put my kid through college with that kind of money. Wait until my arm heals up, I'll walk both the sombitches down to Saigon myself."

"That'd be quite a distance to walk with my boot up your arse," Fritz scoffed to a chorus of laughter from the rest of the team.

Richard felt somewhat melancholy in reflecting on the mood of the team, most thankful that they were alive and kicking after the night before. The local MASH unit was flown in by chopper and were able to tend to the injured without having them evacuated to Saigon. A truckload of beer had been driven up along with a dozen cases of liquor. Yet Richard could not help feel as if the forced camaraderie was as an episode of deja vu. He wondered if this was how it would be for them at the VA Hospital back in the World when all this was over but never gone for good.

He followed Captain Federer into his private office where he had retreated for a fresh pocketful of stogies.

"So did we get any updates on the UFO's?" Richard inquired.

"I've been having one-on-ones with our individual team members," Fred grew brusque. "Word from the top is that we need to keep a lid on that crap. The Pentagon is in the process of compiling information and doing research. What they don't want --- the last thing they want --- is the liberal press getting all over this. We got enough problems out here without all that crazy house crap. And they are serious. If they catch wind of anyone yakking this stuff up, they'll have them shipped back to

Saigon. Chances are they may have to turn their beanie in. And that goes from John Wayne to Barry Sadler, no exceptions."

The meeting adjourned shortly afterward with most of the team retiring to the barracks at Deadwood. Everyone but Fred, Steve, Jim, Richard and Bobby Cuddahy had suffered injury requiring sutures. Word was that Bobby slipped over the fenceline early in the fight and was given up as MIA. Only he reappeared after the UFO incident completely drenched in blood and gore without a scratch on him.

Richard caught the ride on the golf cart with Fritz back to the Castle, after which Y Bro gave him a lift back to Betty's Battalion at Deadwood.

"So they're sweeping that UFO stuff under the carpet."

"Just like your zombie story," Fritz mused.

"If no one saw it, it never happened," Richard growled. "Problem with this is everybody saw it. The team, the cidgees, the puffs, the villagers, everybody. Even the flyboys. That's like two hundred witnesses. How does that work for them?"

"The dinks are a non-factor. With all the demonic stuff going down here, that was just another day. And if anyone talks, the LLDB makes them disappear. Just like the Pentagon can make us disappear. Don't forget the Section Eight thing. They can drug you up, put you in a straitjacket, lock you in a room for one week, and that's all, folks. It's a can they tie to your tail for the rest of your life."

"Whatever," Richard relented as the golf cart stopped and Fritz got off. "So what're you doing today?"

"Spacing out. This thing hurts like a bitch. Feels like somebody ran me through with a hot poker. I'm loading up on painkillers and listening to Wagner."

"Yeah, well, I got that CIA interview. Looks like they got me on their go-fer list."

"Oh, yeah," Fritz stopped and turned toward him. "About the zombie thing."

He lifted his arm, pulled up his sleeve and showed Richard the long gash he suffered during the night of the zombie attack.

"Don't tell anyone," he laughed as he walked off. "Section Eight."

An hour later, Richard sat in the lounge area of Betty's Battalion at a rear table. It was unusually deserted with the team self-medicating at the barracks. He sipped a Guinness as his visitor was served a Cuba Libre by a pretty waitress.

"I am sure that your superiors have placed a gag order against discussions of the recent events," Mr. Uno stirred his drink. The CIA agent met with Richard to discuss an upcoming project, flying up from Saigon shortly after daybreak. "Out of respect for our new relationship, I will answer your question this one time."

"That will be appreciated."

"Any acknowledgment of the existence of these unidentified aircraft creates a dangerous situation for the Pentagon and our government," Uno explained. "If they are products of the Russian or Chinese military industrial complex, it forces us to admit to the global community that they have exceeded our own capabilities. They would have developed weapons that have eclipsed anything we possess. It would be even worse if this is proof of an extraterrestrial community outside our known environment. It would suggest that we are incapable of defending our nation against such a threat. These scenarios are completely unacceptable."

"I don't necessarily agree, but I'll accept it."

"Good. Let us forget about little green men and focus on our problem with the little yellow men."

Uno placed a familiar photo of Chink Abesamis on the table.

"We are quite certain that he is the one circulating the posters and placing the bounty on you and Sgt. Hammer. We also suspect him of masterminding a series of suicide bombings in Saigon over the past months. We have information that he is planning a car bomb attack in Nha Trang. It would be in our mutual interest to have this fellow removed from the face of the earth."

"And what's in it for me, other than getting the posters out of circulation?"

"A month of furlough time, as well as a bonus deposited in your Swiss bank account. We can also arrange an all-expenses paid week in Paris for two."

"Give me the details."

"We've got a good idea of his whereabouts in Nha Trang. Unfortunately he's heavily protected by corrupt government officials and VC sappers (*sleeper cells) so we can't get too close. Plus the fact that the Trang is a heavily-populated resort area, which negates the option of dropping a bomb on him. In all likelihood he's protected by a squad of highly-trained mercenaries. It'll take a well-equipped, equally skilled operative to slip his defenses and take him out."

Mike Abesamis considered his recent work at Vinh Loc Island as a classic takedown, one of his finest. It was a peninsula along the South China seacoast five miles offshore from Hue in Thua Thien Province in I Corps. After the Tet Offensive, MACV moved their forces from the city of Thua Thien to Hue in preventing the enemy from seizing control of the Imperial City.

The islanders were somewhat relieved to have the war machines and the heavily-armed soldiers removed from their idyllic seashore. Only there was a gradual transition from the military personnel to the strangers who began frequenting the isle. At first they came as lone tourists, then made contact and began carousing in pairs. Soon they made further acquaintances and formed groups that flashed money and attracted attention.

The teenagers on the island were solicited and began running errands for the newcomers. They were lavish tippers and soon had the youngsters at their beck and call. The best-looking and most intelligent curried favor and were soon invited to the tables for dinner and cocktail parties. Eventually the gatherings resumed at the cliques' luxury suites and seaside rental properties. The parties lasted until dawn and began to take a toll on the community.

Liquor and drugs were introduced, and hookers were brought in to break the resistance of students and hospitality workers. Absenteeism became rampant and parents called the authorities when their children did not come home by daybreak. The police grew weary of the reports and soon disregarded the truancy. Family crises broke out across the island and the teens were encouraged by their new friends to defy authority. Eventually the situation deteriorated so that neighborhood meetings were organized to address the predicament.

Soon the newcomers scheduled their own meetings to counter those of the community leaders. The teens were introduced to a man named Mike who gave dissertations about the new political trends affecting Vietnam. He gave a historical overview about how the French had colonized the nation after World War II which caused the civil war. After the liberation forces defeated the French, they were replaced by American imperialists who exploited the people of the divided country. South Vietnam was ruled by a weak and inefficient puppet government supported by an older generation who were manipulated to reject liberty, justice and social progress.

Mike recruited leaders to spread the opprobrium among students and teenagers active in the community. They formed groups that met regularly and had access to liquor, sex and drugs after their political rallies. Parents got wind of this and eventually gained possession of the radical propaganda literature. They consulted the village elders who reported the tendentious discussions to community leaders. They, in turn, brought the situation to the attention of political figures who contacted their connections in Saigon.

Government officials determined that they would abide by the wisdom of attracting bees with honey instead of vinegar. They were loathe to draw the attention of the liberal press and radical groups such as the SDS (*Students for a Democratic Society). They decided to deploy their own propaganda organizations to Vinh Loc Island to win the hearts and minds of the adolescents.

They scheduled a Freedom For Vietnam rally at the downtown area just blocks away from the seacoast district. They set up a grandstand and hired two traditional folk bands along with three rock bands. There were guest speakers scheduled, and an ice cream truck and a food truck were brought in to provide free samples throughout the day-long event. It seemed to be a perfect move by the Establishment to counter those of the dissidents.

Only they were checkmated by Mike Abesamis on one of the deadliest days in the island's history. The VC packed the trunk of a Volkswagen with plastic explosives and drove it to within thirty yards of the stage. The bomb was detonated remotely just before the opening ceremony began. Twelve people were killed and dozens injured as the blast ripped through the crowd of attendees. The police launched a manhunt for the killers but found that the highly suspicious strangers had long since vacated the island.

Mike was determined to exceed the expectations of his superiors in Hanoi with this new operation. He and his squad arrived in Nha Trang and set up base at an abandoned warehouse along the outskirts of town. They awaited until a team of drivers brought three trucks to the loading dock at midnight before disappearing.

The first truck was filled with the supplies necessary to complete construction of the items needed to carry out the mission. It left after dropping off the supplies. The second truck was an ice cream truck, the third was a food truck. Only they contained hollowed car transmissions that would be packed with C4 explosives. The transmissions would be encased in shipping crates loaded with construction items such as nuts, bolts, spikes and padlocks. The crates would then be packed in beds of ammonium nitrate fertilizer. They estimated the twin explosions would be powerful enough to level a city block.

Mike had the squad disperse into three fire teams. A four-man unit would keep watch from the roof of the six-story building. The second unit was comprised of the bomb makers. The third group remained on the third floor catwalk along with Mike to coordinate the activity and initiate the operation. They would also be responsible for evacuation procedures if the authorities were to intervene. They all carried walkie-talkies and could maintain constant communication.

The packers were entrusted with wiring the bombs to the ignition devices and the detonators. The transmissions had already been packed, as had the crates and the planting beds. Yet it remained a harrowing task as a false move could cause an explosion and send the warehouse up in flames. The team remained confident as the men were seasoned professionals devoting their careers to bomb making for terrorist organizations. It was 0400 by the time they emerged from the trucks and announced the bombs were primed and ready for use.

"Excellent," Mike rejoiced. "This will make the imperialists think of Vinh Loc as a dumpster fire. When we set these off along the boardwalk district, it will capture headlines from America to Europe."

"Our comrades will do well to double-check and make sure they have left no trace for the Americans to detect," Mike's second-in-command, Bruce Li, cautioned him. "They have the most sophisticated forensics system on the planet. If we are linked to this operation we will be hunted across the globe."

"Who gives a crap?" Joco Van Kamp snarled. The Corsican was a veteran of the French Foreign Legion who defected to the VC after the French debacle at Dien Bien Phu. "We get a million bucks apiece after this job, that lets you live in comfort anywhere on the planet. They'll be like dogs sniffing seats until we're six feet under."

He routinely searched Mike's face for a tell every time he mentioned the money. If he determined a double-cross, he would blow Abesamis' head off without a second thought.

"I'm with Bruce on that," his business partner Chaz Moris ventured. "I don't want to never be able to go back to America or Europe. Money buys lots of things but it'll run out if you got to bribe people every time you take a walk around the block."

"You guys are paranoid," Stiv Seagull, a professional assassin, waved them off. "Don't forget we're in the middle of a war. No matter what kind of terrorist game the VC's playing, the American Army's counting it as military action. You take a target out with a pipe bomb or a mortar round, they're sending in the Marines and looking for body counts. Let me tell you, those guys don't bring handcuffs."

"All of us have been carefully selected for this assignment," Mike reminded them. "Imagine if they were distracted by concerns that we were not doing our jobs keeping guard. That would be a valid reason to worry."

They were standing in a conference room at the rear section on the third floor waiting for the packers to complete their task. Only they were startled by the sight of what appeared to be a sack of garbage falling from the roof onto the pavement at grade level. There was no time to react before a second object dropped from the rooftop. Mike ran out to the catwalk and stared in horror at the sight of two of his riflemen. Their torsos had exploded like melons after falling six stories to the concrete.

"Aiieeee," Mike cried out as the others rushed to see what happened. "They did not slip and fall, that is no accident! Call and check on the others!"

With that, Chaz radioed the roof and got no response. Bruce rushed to a rear window in the corridor and witnessed a similar sight. Two bodies fell from the roof and splattered on the street along the rear of the building. The team considered themselves fortunate that neither of the bodies struck the two getaway vehicles that were parked at the rear entrance.

"Aiyahhh!" Mike pressed his fists against his temples. "There was a squealer, a rat! Somehow they got onto us!"

"Lay off the panic button," Seagull drew his pistol. "I'll go handle this."

"Bad idea," Bruce held out a hand. "You may walk into a trap. Let us wait until they come to us. They can't stay up there all night. We need to provide cover and make sure the packers get the trucks out."

"Or else what?" Seagull demanded.

"If they set those bombs off while the trucks are still in here," Joco stared at him, "there is no 'else what'."

Bruce and Chaz started toward the stairs, only to watch in dismay as the skull of the leader of the packers exploded in a spray of crimson on the grade level.

"They're using silencers," Chaz informed his teammates. "We're not gonna be able to find them unless we see a muzzle flash."

"Why aren't those jackasses drawing their guns?" Seagull fumed.

"If they fire a stray round and it hits one of those payloads, we're all done for," Bruce said tersely.

"Well, those other guys don't have a problem with it," Seagull retorted.

"Obviously that's because whoever sent them don't give a shit if they come back or not," Joco snarled.

"All right, we'll spread out and go down either side of both stairwells," Bruce decided. "Main thing is we get Mike out of here."

"Mike?" Seagull was incredulous.

"You got a better suggestion as to who's gonna get our money for us?" Bruce snapped.

"If one of those trucks explode, you can wave that money goodbye on your way to hell," Joco trotted around the catwalk and headed down the opposite staircase.

As if on cue, a bullet caused the head of the driver of the first truck to spray across the windshield. The victim's death throes caused his legs to flutter as the gunman turned the key in the ignition. The truck rolled forward and slammed into the sheet metal door, which buckled under the impact. Everyone in the building gasped as the contents of the truck were jostled when it bounced off the loading dock.

It resulted in an earth-quaking explosion that tore the front of the building asunder. The two remaining packers were crushed beneath falling debris which bounced off the roof of the second truck. It did not create enough impact to cause an explosion of the volatile material within.

"We need to bail," Seagull growled. "The second truck's trapped in there, we can't get it past all that crap. The five of us are all that's left. We can live to die another day."

"There may be a chance we can grab one of these attackers," Bruce insisted. "We can find out who sent them and how they got onto us."

"Stiv and I can get Mike downstairs and get the cars ready for takeoff," Joco suggested. "I'm thinking this may be a fire team. They would've made their presence known if they came in force. At the least they would've tried to save one of the trucks for analysis to try and identify the bomb maker."

"I agree," Chaz said to Mike. "If there's six or less of them, Bruce and I are more than enough to take them out. This may be a lone wolf who got wind of this and got the jump on us. Even if he brought his buddies, they'll wish they all stayed home."

"Don't risk your lives, you're too valuable," Mike instructed him. "If faced with a superior force, put bullets in the remaining truck. We can retreat under cover of the explosion."

Chaz and Bruce looked at each other in bemusement before heading along the catwalk to find the intruder. They knew that setting off the explosives would create an blast that they would not escape. Yet leaving it intact for capture by the Americans would compromise their entire operation. Their only hope was to kill these intruders before they took steps to destroy all evidence.

Bruce darted to the right, trotting around in hopes of detecting movement amidst the bomb damage. Chaz signaled Bruce as he moved left along the catwalk, almost immediately hidden from sight by the acrid clouds of smoke rising from the grade level.

Once Chaz disappeared, Bruce immediately detected movement on his peripherals from his right side. He spun reflexively and threw a side kick that was blocked by the intruder. Bruce followed up with a spinning back kick that forced his opponent back. Only his larger adversary grabbed his foot and wrenched it into an ankle lock. The man expertly torqued the left leg before dropping his weight down, twisting it to distend the hamstring. The debilitating pain left Bruce vulnerable to a series of stomps and kicks to the head. The attacker dropped to one knee and grabbed Bruce's windpipe, twisting and wrenching until Bruce was no more.

Richard Mc Cain rose to meet Chaz Moris, who came rushing back upon seeing the altercation. Bruce and Chaz had been partners for over a decade, and Moris gave vent to rage as he charged at Richard with a series of front kicks. Richard parried the blows until Chaz paused for a microsecond to adjust his balance. Richard surged forth with a left jab that was as a battering ram against the smaller foe. He continued to charge and threw a wicked right cross that caused Chaz's eyes to roll. Moris twisted his body and reached inside his blazer for his shoulder holster. Richard tackled him to the metal catwalk and straddled him, gripping his throat as he did to Bruce. Within a minute Chaz's windpipe was crushed.

Outside the building, Mike was checking his watch frantically as the threesome awaited for Bruce and Chaz to return. He knew that authorities would learn of the explosion and begin deploying at any moment. It would take them fifteen minutes to arrive from downtown at worst, which gave the team little time to escape unhindered.

"What the hell is taking those two?" Seagall saw Mike looking at his watch. "The cops'll be here any minute."

He was answered by the sound of breaking glass as a body hurtled from the third floor window. Mike and Stiv were shocked at the sight of Bruce's corpse bouncing off the top of the yellow Trans Am and rolling off onto the ground.

Richard had hooked up a bungee cord along the roof ledge after having killed the gunmen on the rooftop. It was a gimmick he had perfected with Army paratroopers at Fort Benning while he was training stateside. He vaulted out the window behind Bruce's body and dropped to the sidewalk. Only when the cord stretched to the max, he sprang away and landed alongside Stiv. He had already drawn his foot-long stiletto and slit Seagall's throat with a mighty slash.

Joco Van Kamp was already exiting the Corvette behind the Trans Am and charged directly at Richard. He was close to Richard's height though the Missourian had the weight advantage. He threw a volley of right roundhouse kicks which forced Richard back against the wall. Richard tried to counter with the stiletto but Joco was able to parry the thrust, He threw a left roundhouse before slamming himself against Richard in shoving the knife hand so the tip of the blade pierced Richard's left bicep.

Richard dropped the knife, throwing a left jab though the wound burned as fire. Joco easily parried the blow and threw a front kick that snapped Richard's head back. He slowly sank on one knee to the pavement as Joco dropped back into a horse stance, preparing to launch a thunderous roundhouse in finishing his opponent off. Only it positioned him so he was entirely unprepared as Richard scooped up the stiletto. He drove it up with all his might into Joco's crotch, piercing his pelvis and slicing into his bowels.

Richard heard the squealing of tires and the roar of the engine as the Trans Am lurched away from the curb and peeled off down the street. He cursed softly as he rushed to the Corvette and slid in behind the wheel. He was sure that the gangsters left the key in the ignition. His hopes were realized as he gunned the engine and set off in pursuit of Abesamis.

The Pontiac roared down an unmarked road that ran parallel to the city limits due north. The sports car was moving at 100 MPH, and Richard realized that it was as fast as Abesamis could drive. These cars went to a max of 140 MPH, and it was a speed Richard had only driven a small number of times. Hitting a curve or dodging an obstacle required considerable skill, and losing control could be fatal. He decided he would stay on Abesamis' tail and wait from him to run out of gas. He wanted this guy alive. He knew he would be transferring the deed to a gold mine of intel if he could bring him in to Uno and the CIA.

They were streaking along for nearly a half hour until the inevitable happened. Abesamis began swerving wildly, and Richard pumped the brakes as he watched the Trans Am go into a spin and career off the road onto a slope from the roadway. He slowed to a halt and rolled carefully down the incline so that he could retake the high ground if necessary.

He saw Abesamis exit the vehicle and begin running across the sward to a treeline in the distance. It was as a confidence boost in knowing Abesamis would not be able to negotiate the woods as easily as Richard could. If he decided to play hide and seek, daybreak would be a major handicap. The cops would be scouring this area once the truck bombs were discovered at the warehouse. Helicopters and bloodhounds would easily finish this job.

It was a typical jungle treeline with thick foliage along the interior. There was a mist rising from the compost that impeded visibility. Richard moved forth, treading on the balls of his feet as he proceeded. He was dressed in black with a long-sleeved nylon shirt and cargo pants along with combat boots. His only weapon had been the lost stiletto. He knew most of the combat was going to be hand-to-hand, and a firearm would have been a handicap in such situations. The silencer-fitted pistols had been turned against their owners. They had been killed by their own hands.

He slipped between two trees and was suddenly hammered over the back of the head with a blow that dropped him to his knees. Everything was a blur, and he was staggered so that he offered no resistance as his arms were pulled behind his back and his wrists bound.

"So," Abesamis grinned as he shoved Richard to a sitting position against a tree. "At last we meet. My comrades will have a reconnaissance team in this area within the hour. We had already devised a contingency plan should such a thing as this had occurred. But first you will tell me how you found us, and where is the rest of your team."

"I just followed the smell," Richard replied. "And as you can see, I didn't need anyone else."

With that, Abesamis slapped him as hard as he could across the face.

"You bastard," he cried. "Those were trusted comrades and loyal friends you ambushed. Not only will I collect the bounty on your head, but I will turn you over to my interrogators. I will watch them reduce you to a quivering pulp begging for death."

"Yeah?" Richard sneered. "Well, I can make you squirt a few right now."

With that he hooked his foot around the back of Abesamis' heel. He then shot his right boot out and slammed Mike's instep. The man squealed as he tripped and fell back on his rump. He gasped in pain before stumbling to regain his feet. He attacked Richard in a blind rage, pummeling him wildly with both fists. Richard lowered his head and accepted the blows as a parent indulging a spoiled child having a tantrum.

"Motherfucka! I kill you!" he choked.

Abesamis lurched drunkenly to retrieve the tree limb he used to knock Richard senseless. He had tossed it aside in order to bind Richard's wrists with thick vines he found nearby. The limb landed in a marsh a few feet away where it stood curiously erect. Mike went to retrieve it but ventured only a short distance before his boot sank nearly a foot deep. He tried to pull loose but sank up to his knee with the other leg. Within seconds both men realized Abesamis was caught in quicksand.

"How do you like that?" Richard chortled. "If your team doesn't show up in a few minutes, they won't find a trace of your slope head in all that muck. Ever see Alfalfa on the *Little Rascals?* Twirl up a strand on top and maybe they can pull you out."

"Help! Help!" Abesamis screamed.

Both men caught their breath as a figure emerged from the foliage behind Mike. They stared in wonder as a diminutive priest clad in versicolored ceremonial robes made his way across the mud. He reminded Richard of the little white men on the Minefield. His large withered head sat on a spindly neck, his frail legs barely able to support his scrawny body.

"Where are you going, priest?" Abesamis cried as the priest swept toward Richard as if Mike was not there. "You are a proud yellow man, just as I. We celebrate Asian pride. Power to the people! I --- *ai ai ai!*"

Mike reached out and grabbed the priest's legs, only to have his hands flounder in air as if he had tried to grasp a hologram. His arms went right through the ectoplasm as the wraith continued to where Richard was tied. The priest quickly untied Richard's hands, then stepped towards the brush and disappeared.

"Well, ain't that a bitch," Richard rubbed his wrists, rising to his feet. "Now, I've seen some women pay good money to have faeries put mud packs on their faces. Maybe it'll do something for all that acne. So long, Chink."

Richard darted back through the treeline and straight to the yellow Corvette. He gunned the engine and began streaking back to Nha Trang. Only within minutes, the VC recon unit made it in time to find Mike and pull him from the quicksand.

"Our agents inside the police force reported that the warehouse is crawling with cops as we speak," the leader of the unit advised Mike as the disheveled man sat on a log to recover. "This is a sorry day for the Cause. The upside is that you are safe, comrade."

"So this ugly dog gambled his life to try and take you," another man studied a poster of Richard they had brought along. The CIA informed the Special Branch at Nha Trang that Richard was onsite when news broke over the warehouse explosion. The VC agents were quick to advise the recon unit in turn.

"I'm sure he'll have nothing to do with you again," the leader grinned.

"No, no, no," Abesamis grinned evilly. "We've only just begun."

10

SATELLITE OF LOVE

Richard was taken to Saigon after being intercepted by Special Branch officers. He was debriefed by CIA agents before being sent back to Dong Ha. He slept in and did not get back to normal until the following day.

He kept reliving the events of the previous night, and it had his mind racing a hundred miles an hour. He thought of the priest, another lost soul wandering the earth. Was he killed at his temple? Was he beheaded so that he was in eternal search to rejoin his head to his interred corpse? Did some devil paint a green cross on his face? Or was it just another demonic curse these people believed in?

He was just as fascinated by Chink Abesamis, who got the xenophobic nickname in being a Chinese national. What made him buy into this game? He obviously wasn't cut out for this. Did he have family here that was traumatized or shattered by this war? Did he see an elderly relative abused? Was there a young male friend murdered? Had a female family member been raped or killed?

Fritz once told him a story of his father's unit being

withdrawn from a Russian village where the SS was conducting cleanup operations. The Jews were being herded onto livestock trucks to be transported to concentration camps. He never forgot the uncomprehending and frightened looks, as the heartrending gaze of the puppy in the gas chamber. Fritz could not help but compare it to those of the villagers being taken from their ancestral homes and taken to a fortified hamlet. Taken from a place that was all they knew to a place they knew nothing of.

"I'm a Jew now," Fritz would raise a glass of melancholy.

There were also the accusations of Henry Geronimo that echoed from the time/space continuum.

Did he like killing?

He remembered the time-worn admonition of the hit men, the serial killers that fascinated him as an amateur criminologist in high school. It was back when he thought of being a cop and saving the community before he dreamed of saving the world. He remembered how it was said that the first kill was always the hardest. Afterward it got easier until, over time, you grew comfortably numb. His first one was at a distance under cover of night. It was some time later before he saw the lights go out in his enemy's eyes. An enemy trying to cut his heart out with a hunting knife.

The twelve men he sent to hell were stone cold killers. They were putting together truck bombs that would kill men, women and children. Every one of them save for the lone Chinaman, Bruce Li, were Caucasians. How did they justify it? Was it for love of money? Perhaps it was how he came to despise the hit men who wrote their memoirs and glorified their lifestyles. They spoke of honor and loyalty just as Fritz's Dad honored the SS and his son honored the Special Forces. Yet at some point, one ends up taking the responsibility of representing the organization entire.

They said history was written by the victors. America would forever portray the Native American as savages who burned wagon trains, scalped the pioneers and ambushed US Cavalry patrols. The Trail of Tears was always depicted as an unfortunate anomaly. Germany would never erase the guilt of the SS. Great Britain would forever be reminded of the Troubles in Northern Ireland. He remembered the question posed by the spirit of Henry Geronimo. Suppose America lost this war? Perhaps the posters of Richard and Fritz would hang in the rooms of Vietnamese teenagers of the next generation. Like Butch Cassidy and the Sundance Kid.

He remembered the family reunion at the Lake of the Ozarks, the one time the Mc Cains and the Brookses came together when Jake was thirteen and Richard was ten. They rented out a campground along with a dozen bungalows and a double-wide trailer that accommodated over two dozen relatives. Most had not seen each other since the wedding of Johnny and Maryanne, and many would never meet again.

Four generations were represented during an afternoon of fishing. Henry Geronimo, the grandfather of Maryanne Brooks, was there along with Eamon Mc Cain, the father of Johnny Mc Cain. Johnny and his son Richard knew it was a time none of them would ever forget. Eamon, a native of Belfast, exchanged stories with Henry of times and days forgotten. Johnny spent as much time as he could with his sons but knew this was something special.

"Remember this day," Johnny patted his son's shoulder. "You'll make us proud."

Were they proud of him now?

He took his shower and eschewed the bottle of Vicodin that beckoned from the medicine cabinet. He played some football but loved playing hockey, and regularly indulged in wrestling, boxing, karate and judo. He got used to the bumps and bruises but was totally unprepared for getting shot and stabbed. He had not yet broken anything, but there were enough cracks and chips to have gotten him a space at the curbside had he been a set of chinaware. He only popped pills when it would have been impossible to walk otherwise. Recreational drugs were not beyond the pale, but he disdained the use of crutches be they physical or psychological.

He stepped before the full-length mirror as he dressed and took a long hard look. His body was covered with the scars of the game. He had been shot, stabbed, beaten with blunt instruments, cut, burned, and thrown from high places. There were explosions, car wrecks, overturned trucks and helicopter crashes. He would, with God's blessing, celebrate his twenty-fifth birthday on Halloween. What would he look like at thirty?

Thoughts of Laura Mueller crept into his mind. He tried not to fantasize of marrying her, of buying her a home, of having a family. Not only might he jinx himself, but the loss of such hope would be unbearable. Yet what would she think of seeing a body as scarred as this? Would she accept this until death did them part?

He pulled on his black T-shirt, his green cargo pants and his combat boots. He flexed his muscles and decided he might get away with it by keeping the lights out at night. He wasn't hard on the eyes otherwise. Loki was always giving him the look, and he knew they always asked for him at Betty's Battalion. He didn't do too shabby in Saigon before Laura came along.

He negotiated the speed bump with Laura during their first date when she asked if he had killed anyone. He admitted he had, and she naively asked how many. She was too beautiful for him to reject the question.

"Two hundred?" she mused. "That's a lot of guys."

"Yeah."

"So," she could not resist, and he loved her sense of humor forever after. "Did you throw a bomb in a movie theater?"

"Something like that."

For some strange reason it made him think of the time the Crazy Eight came up to thank him for his service during a patrol run. In a different place and time he would have gotten at least a Bronze Star. They chose to reward him with a goat which they had on a tether. He thanked them individually, and they profusely expressed their personal thanks for saving their lives. They asked if he would like assistance in drawing, quartering and barbecuing the goat. He politely declined.

Shortly thereafter he arrived at Dogpatch with the goat. He approached a group of children playing in the kiddie park and told them they could have the goat for a petting zoo. They were jubilant as he departed, hugging and petting their new friend. Only he returned the next day to find a goat's hide drying on the wall of a home near the park. There was a carcass on a barbecue spit, and a group of children were sitting around enjoying what he presumed was Goat's Head Soup.

Some things never changed.

Before he left the Shanty, he stopped and stared at the grim-faced young man in the mirror with the sad yet stoic eyes. He wondered if it was the same fellow he recognized.

Could he love?

He squinted as he stepped out into the morning sunlight and saw Fritz sitting on the landing at the Castle. He came over as Fritz stood and stretched, grabbing his black cane with the silver wolf's head handle. Fritz hobbled over as they took the short walk to Deadwood. He had dismissed his gold cart driver, deciding the walk was good exercise.

"How's the leg?"

"Did you think I was just practicing my Charlie Chaplin routine?"

"Kinda dead at Betty's the last time I was there."

"Yeah," Fritz nodded. "Uncle Fred furloughed most of the Team. He's still got Steve playing go-fer and Bobby doing god-knows-what. I'm pretty sure Jim's still up on the Ledge doing the peace pipe thing."

"So I take it Fred's still here."

"Yeah. As a matter of fact, he's finishing up the paperwork for the green light on the Red Cross field trip."

"Field trip?"

"Seems like Saigon approved a special convoy on a goodwill run. They've got some volunteer nurses coming up with ice cream and cakes, like a State Fair. It's supposed to be a celebration over us holding the fort. The gooks'll be the ones enjoying the benefit, And maybe some lucky bastard."

"Yeah? Who might that be?"

"Well, it's definitely not me," Fritz sniggered.

They walked onto the clearing just as a Red Cross truck arrived. They watched as the rear tailgate dropped and a staircase lowered. To their surprise and delight, a gaggle of nurses made their way down the steps as a squad of ARVN riflemen appeared as an escort for the VIP's.

The last one came forth and spotted Richard standing ten yards away. She was a beautiful woman, an angel of light clad in a knee-high white dress uniform. She knew she was looking good, a calendar girl come to life. She struck the pose, standing hands on hips with feet spread apart. She was enjoying him having a long look.

"*Laura!*"

"Fred said there were special guests aboard," Fritz grinned, feeling glad for his friend.

"What kind of guys could be this lucky?" Richard was flabbergasted.

"Guys like you, Mickey," Fritz smiled as he walked away.

He saw Loki standing in front of Path Three, gazing wistfully at Richard and Laura. Fritz caught her eye and nodded in the direction of the Castle. She smiled and resignedly headed toward Path Five. It was said that misery loves company.

Laura impulsively ran toward him and came to a halt at arm's length, gazing into his moonstruck eyes.

"I told you my Dad worked at the Bank of Duluth. He just so happens to be a Vice President and a member of the Chamber of Commerce. I told him about us, and I mentioned my nursing degree and the Red Cross thing. He pulled some strings and, *ta da*. I'll be here for the weekend."

At once they fell into each others' arms, their lips meeting in an everlasting kiss. They were swept into another dimension where a new world was forming. It was the center of an embryonic galaxy where stars exploded, black holes emitted showers of celestial light, and cherubim and seraphim heralded the beginning of a new age...

He could love.

Oh yes...

...he could love.

~~END~~

Dear reader,

We hope you enjoyed reading *Fox*. Please take a moment to leave a review, even if it's a short one. Your opinion is important to us.

Discover more books by John Reinhard Dizon at https://www.nextchapter.pub/authors/john-reinhard-dizon

Want to know when one of our books is free or discounted? Join the newsletter at http://eepurl.com/bqqB3H

Best regards,

John Reinhard Dizon and the Next Chapter Team

Printed in Great Britain
by Amazon

16493570R00098